**Powerful, Loyal, Unforgettable
Follow the Titans
As they find true love**

The Tycoon's Vacation

D1531241

THE TYCOON'S VACATION

Baby for the Billionaire – Book Two
By Melody Anne

COPYRIGHT

© 2011 Melody Anne

Printed and published in the United States of America.
Published by Gossamer Publishing
Cover art by Exclusive Publishing Company

Salt Lake City, Utah

Look for us online at:
www.exclusivepublishing.com
Email: Info@exclusivepublishing.com

DEDICATION

This book is dedicated to my amazing husband,
Marty. Thank you for all your time and patience,
and most of all for helping me research

NOTE FROM THE AUTHOR

I loved writing this story. How many times as a teenager did I dream of going to an exotic place and finding the man of my dreams? Too many times to count. There is something incredibly sexy about fantasies, and this book is a fantasy come to life.

I found my true love in my own backyard, but I choose to imagine it as a little more exotic. ☺ Love is amazing and wonderful, and the fighting along the way is exciting.

Thank you again to all of my incredible fans. Thank you for your reviews and comments; I hope they continue to pour in. I do read each and every message you send. I will continue to do so no matter how long it takes. I know I can't do what I love without you, and I appreciate your help every single day.

I hope you're enjoying the Titan Cousins. Here we go on Book Two.

Melody Anne

BOOKS BY MELODY ANNE

BILLIONAIRE BACHELORS

*The Billionaire Wins the Game

*The Billionaire's Dance

*The Billionaire Falls

*The Billionaire's Marriage Proposal

*Blackmailing the Billionaire

*Runaway Heiress

*The Billionaire's Final Stand

*Unexpected Treasure

*Hidden Treasure

*Holiday Treasure

BABY FOR THE BILLIONAIRE

+The Tycoon's Revenge

+The Tycoon's Vacation

+The Tycoon's Proposal

+The Tycoon's Secret

+The Lost Tycoon

RISE OF THE DARK ANGEL

-Midnight Fire – Rise of the Dark Angel – Book One

-Midnight Moon – Rise of the Dark Angel – Book Two

-Midnight Storm – Rise of the Dark Angel – Book Three

-Midnight Eclipse – Rise of the Dark Angel – Book Four – **Coming Soon**

SURRENDER

=Surrender – Book One

=Submit – Book Two

=Seduced – Book Three

=Scorched – Book Four

FORBIDDEN SERIES

+Bound – Book One

+Broken – Book Two – **Coming December 15th**

HEROES SERIES

-Safe in his arms – Novella – *Baby it's Cold Outside* Anthology

-Her Unexpected Hero – Book One – **Releases Feb 28th 2015**

-Who I am with you – Novella – **Coming soon**

-Her Hometown Hero – Book Two – **Releases June 2015**

PROLOGUE

YOU DON'T KNOW what you're missing out on, Drew. I've never been as happy as I am now. I love you and Ryan, you know that, but having a wife and children is unlike anything you can imagine. I feel...I don't know...complete." Derek spoke to his cousin as they sat by the pool, having a drink and catching up.

"I think Jasmine is about the most perfect woman in this universe, but marriage is for you — not me. I like being a bachelor, and I want it to stay that way. I believe in freedom. Why should I settle down with just one lady when I can have a new one on my arm anytime I want?" Drew flashed a wicked smile. So what if he sometimes felt a longing for something more? The grass is always greener, no? He had a great life and saw no reason to change anything.

"I used to feel the same way — until Jasmine came back into my life. Now I just think of all the wasted years we could have been together," Derek said.

Drew winced at the pain in his cousin's voice. Derek had finally married his childhood sweetheart, but circumstances had kept them apart for ten years, and Drew knew all too well how much Derek suffered when he thought about the years forever lost.

"I think I'm just restless because I need a vacation," Drew said. "I've been working nonstop lately and it's time to pick one of my resorts and go soak up some sun and lie on the beach. I'm sure I can find a pretty lady or three to enjoy the time with," he said.

Drew had always believed in keeping things simple when it came to women. That had always been enough for him, so he figured the restlessness really was just too much hard work. The old saying seemed to be quite fitting — all work and no play...

"What's with the serious expressions? What on earth are you boys discussing?" Jasmine asked. She walked out, carrying her beautiful baby girl, and Drew immediately held out his arms to take her. He'd fallen head over heels in love with his niece, and he could even imagine himself with a few of his own children someday. Scratch that. Babies usually came with a wife, and that was a no-go.

"Drew was just talking about chasing tail," Derek said as he grabbed Jasmine around the waist and settled her onto his lap. She laughed and bent down to kiss him. Drew cleared his throat to remind them he was still there.

"Sorry, Drew," Jasmine mumbled; a pretty blush stole over her features.

"Want to babysit?" Derek asked, though it wasn't really a question. He also wasn't the least bit sorry. Before Drew had a chance to say anything, Derek rose with Jasmine still in his arms and carried her off. Her feeble protests faded as the two disappeared into the house.

Britney's irresistible blue eyes and toothless smile tugged at Drew's heart. He blew raspberries on her stomach, which made her giggle and pat his face.

"I know your parents are a bit nutty, but you have to love them anyway," he said. He didn't feel foolish telling her things, even though she had no idea what he was saying. He found himself babysitting for a long time before the happy couple returned.

He raised his brows at his cousin, who just shrugged as if to say he couldn't help himself. Jasmine apologized for her husband's behavior and took Britney back so she could get the child ready for bed. Drew's arms felt instantly empty.

"I'm going to take off now since my presence here is obviously not needed," Drew said with a huge smile.

"Hey, you know you're always wanted here," Derek told him.

Drew knew that his cousin meant those words. All three of the cousins had been only children, but it had never seemed that way. Having Derek and Ryan was even better than having siblings. Their bond was unbreakable.

"I know," Drew said. "That's why I keep coming back. I'm going to take everyone's advice, though, and take that vacation. I'm sure once I get away from work, I'll feel better, and can get back to myself."

"Don't stay away too long. You know how quickly Britney is growing up." Derek walked Drew to the door.

"I can't believe how quickly she's growing. It seems like only yesterday she was born, and look at her, already a few months old. I won't be gone long — she'd miss me too much. Plus, I'm thinking it's time to start slowing down. Traveling the world isn't holding the same appeal it used to when I first started building these resorts. Now that you're all settled down, I look forward to coming back. I think it's your wife's cooking. I swear I've put on twenty pounds," he said, while rubbing his flat stomach.

"I understand. I'm going to have to go to the tailor to let all my pants out." Derek rubbed his own six-pack abs. They shook hands and Drew walked out. He sat in his car and gazed at his cousin's home with the warm lights inviting a person to step inside. He shook his head as he started his silver Bugatti Veyron, listening to the 1200 horsepower engine roar to life. He grinned as he started down the road. Yeah, he'd get back to his normal self. Kids and luxury vehicles didn't go hand in hand.

As he headed to the airport, he phoned his pilot and knew his jet would be fueled and ready by the time he arrived. Some sun and surf would wash all thoughts of marriage and children away. He simply wasn't the marrying kind, not the way Derek was.

Once inside his jet, Drew looked around at what he had and sighed. Life was good. Sure, Derek's suggestion that something was missing niggled at him somewhere in the back of his mind, but he knew better.

After the plane got airborne, he sipped his drink and laid his head back against the seat. As he closed his eyes and took a few breaths, the world seemed to slow down. *Yeah*, he thought, *this is what I needed*. After a few days of nothing but surf, sun, and sand, everything would return to normal.

CHAPTER ONE

TRINITY LAY ON an oversized towel, a sigh of ecstasy escaping her lips. The sun shining down on her closed eyelids was melting the tension from her tight shoulders, and she imagined herself floating away on the crystal-clear water that lapped on the beach.

This was the first impulsive thing she'd done in her life. She'd always been the personification of the word responsible, dammit. But after being walked all over by yet another boyfriend, she had packed one bag, hopped on a jet, and ended up on a secluded island off the north coast of Spain. The last leg of her journey, on a small charter aircraft, had given her spectacular views of the Mediterranean Sea. She'd been unable to take her eyes away from the window as the aircraft circled the island before landing in this paradise.

To come to this mega-expensive luxury resort with all the amenities and more, she'd spent every dime she'd saved carefully over the last ten years. So what if she'd be eating ramen noodles for the next year? This place was worth it.

Her life had been flipped upside down a few days ago, and

she'd just snapped. She'd always been the people pleaser in her group of friends and in the few romantic relationships she'd been in. She was stubborn to a fault with herself, always setting high goals to achieve, but when it came to others she was a pushover. She vowed never to let that happen again.

The one upside to her last relationship was that she was now feeling the warmth of the sun. She stood up and headed toward the inviting water. Though she'd been trying hard not to think about her ex, the jerk kept invading her thoughts. Yet another relationship gone wrong.

Trinity had been with her supposedly straight-laced boyfriend for six months and, just a few days before, had felt it was time to take the next step. One thing about him that had impressed her so much was his willingness to wait for her to be ready to go to bed with him.

As she stood in front of her mirror, looking at the way the dress hugged her body, she took a deep breath for courage. Excitement pulsed through her as she thought about the two of them entwined in a night of lovemaking. She'd never been one to have casual affairs — she'd taken that final step with only two other men, and the result in both cases was utter disaster. Was sex to be a chore to her, not a pleasure? So far, it had felt that way. But things just had to change with this man. They got along perfectly. And if he didn't cause her stomach to quiver, maybe that was just the silly hyperbole of the romance novels she'd read. More likely, when they finally got down to the act of love, she'd feel the explosion she'd searched for.

Trinity had the key to his place; he'd given it to her the month before so she could take care of his plants while he was on a business trip. She'd forgotten she still had it, but when she arrived at his door, she was grateful. She had her arms full of every seduction tool she could think of — candles, lotions, oils…even whipped cream. Her face lit up with a smile as she turned the doorknob.

It was such a cliché. Yes, she opened the door, her heart racing with anticipation, only to find the creep in bed with his secretary. He begged Trinity to stay, while the naked woman next to him stared daggers at her. It was almost laughable — it would have been, had she not been so crushed. He promised it was a one-time thing, that he temporarily lost his mind. One thought broke through her disbelief: *pathetic*.

As she'd walked out the door, she vowed she was done with businessmen for good. She'd always been the perfect girlfriend to these assholes, doing their laundry, cleaning their homes, and being at their beck and call. Is that what they saw in her? A poor sap? Powerful men seemed to expect servants instead of wives.

Well, she was done being the girl everyone could depend on. She was done always playing it safe. She was certainly done with being a doormat. She was now doing what she wanted, in an island paradise and blessedly without any male companion to drag her down.

Trinity dove into the water and swam until her arms started to ache, and she still couldn't wash away the thoughts of her last couple of days.

She'd gotten into her car and driven back to her boring, beige apartment. As she looked around in disgust, she felt a violent shift inside, a tearing, a shattering — and a metamorphosis. The old Trinity was gone.

Enough of being responsible. She dashed to her computer and started searching the Internet for exotic resorts. When she found a brand-new resort off the coast of Spain that had everything she wanted and more, she booked her ticket and hit the mall to buy a new bikini.

When she returned home after the stores closed, she realized to her complete amazement that she hadn't cried. She'd shed not a single tear for the man she'd spent months with. It was suddenly clear. She didn't love him, and she certainly didn't need him. She was free of him and of her old, staid self. She had a hard time falling asleep, she was so excited over her impulsive trip.

Her first night on the island, a spectacular sunset had triggered the first tears she'd shed for a long time. The sheer beauty of colors splashed across the sky caused more emotion in her than any man ever had. She was exhausted as she climbed back up to her room. Finally, the last couple of days caught up to her, and she fell into a deep, healing sleep.

For a few seconds after she woke up that morning, she'd been confused about where she was. She'd sipped a few too many margaritas in the outdoor bar the night before. Once it all came back to her, she couldn't keep the smile from her face. She'd slipped on her incredibly daring bikini, and then headed to the resort's private beach.

Trinity snapped back to the present and realized how far out she'd swum. She was a good swimmer, but she was so far from shore, the resort looked like a hut. She turned around and started heading back in. Emptying her mind of all thought, she focused only on the warmth from the sun and the coolness of the glorious water. She felt no stress, no feelings of regret, and no doubt she'd made the right choice.

She felt only good things — until something crashed into her head. There was a moment of shooting pain, and then blackness. Her last thought before she sank beneath the surface of the water was that her room was nonrefundable.

CHAPTER TWO

DREW CLIMBED OUT of his jet and let the island's intense heat soak through him. Yes, he was ready to change clothes and hit the waves. He climbed into the golf cart waiting for him and smiled broadly. This was no place like home.

He swept down the small hill, away from the even smaller airport, and grinned as his resort came into view. He loved his job — he loved finding the perfect spot of paradise to build an exquisite work of architecture. He was involved from the beginning, choosing the land, the exact placement on that land, and then taking part in the creation of every nook and cranny of his one-of-a-kind design. Not one of his resorts looked the same, and he was proud of that fact. His loyal customers could go to a different one each year and get a new and unique experience.

He walked in through the employee entrance, watching as the staff moved around, performing efficiently in the clean space. It took several moments for someone to notice him.

"Hello, Mr. Titan. I was surprised when I saw your jet land,"

John, his head of security, said as he approached with his hand out.

"Hi, John. I'm here on vacation. Let everyone know that I'm not the boss for the next several days. If there's a problem, deal with it like you normally would if I'm not here," Drew said. He enjoyed the look of surprise on John's face. The man's workaholic boss wasn't playing true to type!

"Of course, sir," John replied. He quickly walked away to inform the staff of Drew's request, and Drew went to his suite and changed.

It took him no time to grab his board and start paddling out into the deep water. The waves were too mellow for his taste, and he'd have to go farther than usual. He was OK with that, though. Nothing was going to upset his perfect mood.

As he moved farther out, he felt every last ounce of stress drift away into the sea... Bang! Damn. He'd just hit something. He turned his head to try to find out what it was, and he barely caught a glimpse of a body as it sank below the water's surface.

"What the hell?" He dove off his board. No one was ever out this far unless they were surfing. He supposed the person's board could have gotten away, but he didn't see one floating anywhere without a rider.

He caught the person — it was a woman! — before she sank too far. He threw her on his board and quickly paddled back to shore, where he immediately began CPR. He was panicked until she choked up some water and started to breathe again. That's when he finally allowed himself to sit back and assess the situation.

She looked up at him through bloodshot eyes and groaned. Her hand immediately reached for her head, where he could already see a large lump forming. Drew's eyes widened and his body tightened at the sight of her. Sheesh. How pathetic.

He'd just about killed the girl, and he certainly had no business gawking at her as if she were some bikini model on display for his pleasure.

She was spectacular, though, in an understated girl-next-door kind of way. She had long blond hair that was currently plastered over her face. Her emerald eyes were staring at him with confusion, and even though she was growing visibly worried, there was still a sparkle deep within their depths that was holding him captive to her gaze.

Her body was toned and yet curvy and feminine with hips just the right size for his hands to hold onto. What was it with these thoughts? He shook his head and focused on her medical needs.

She was far too pale to be so unprotected on these beaches. He could already see a red tint all over her fair skin. The burn was going to bother her in the morning if she didn't get plenty of lotion on. Hell, probably even if she did.

His body went into overdrive at the thought of rubbing lotion across her smooth skin. He could almost picture his hands gliding down the contour of her waist, rubbing across her gently rising hip, and over the lushness of her backside... Drew groaned and pulled himself together.

What the hell is wrong with me? he shouted in his head. The poor woman had almost drowned — his fault — and he was mentally taking her on a public beach. A stiff drink and a night of unattached sex would fix him, he decided — just not the woman he'd hurt.

They'd still exchanged no words when he reached down and lifted her into his arms. Several people rushed forward as they tuned in to what had happened.

"Can we help?" Two guys were standing next to Drew, looking from him to the woman.

"I'll get her inside, thanks," Drew replied before easily carrying her to the resort.

With every step he took, the swell of her breasts bounced against his chest, causing his breathing to quicken as if he were running a marathon. He hoped like hell that she thought he was just overexerted instead of overexcited. Damn. Even the scent of her hair was driving him wild.

Her tiny bikini didn't hide much from his view and he wanted to move the top those last couple of inches. It was almost a burning need to see if her peaks were a soft pink or a dark red. He groaned aloud as he tried to think of anything but hot sex with the stranger in his arms. Damn, he wasn't a horny teenager, but a grown man. He sure as hell wasn't acting like it.

"What happened?" She spoke in a scratchy voice.

Drew jumped a little at her first words. He was so lost in his own fantasies, he hadn't even bothered to explain anything to her. As he watched her flinch from the pain of speaking, his guilt tore him away from his insane lust for his victim.

"I hit you with my surfboard. You went under the water, but only for a few seconds before I got you out. I performed CPR, and I'm sure your throat's tender, but we're going to the first-aid station to see if there's any damage." As he spoke, he carried her into the air-conditioned building. She immediately began to shiver and his eyes were once again drawn to her now beaded nipples. He picked up his pace.

He reached the first-aid station, laid her down, and quickly found a blanket to cover her. It was both for her benefit, and his. The doctor was there within minutes, as he kept one on call at the resort twenty-four hours a day. Too many things could go wrong, even in paradise, and they were very isolated. He wanted his guests to know that help was always available, night or day.

The woman drifted to sleep before the doctor could begin his examination. Drew looked on in concern. Head trauma victims were supposed to stay awake, weren't they?

"Should we wake her up?"

"Why don't you tell me what happened? Then I'll know if she should be awake or not," the doctor replied as he looked at the nasty lump first.

Drew explained what had happened while the doctor examined her thoroughly. After what seemed like forever, he finally turned back to Drew.

"I think she'll be just fine. Her head is going to hurt pretty badly, but other than that, there doesn't seem to be permanent damage. Her pupils are fine, and I don't think a CT scan is called for now. Still, she shouldn't be left alone tonight, so if no one is with her, she needs to stay in the hospital or with someone watching her until morning. With a head injury, she has to be woken every couple of hours to be safe. She doesn't have to get up, but we want to make sure she doesn't slip into a coma or to see whether she develops other symptoms of a bad concussion — here's a handout with a list of them. She also needs to rub this aloe lotion on her skin. I'm actually more concerned about her burn than anything else."

The resort's biggest medical issue was always sunburned clients. They weren't used to the intense heat of the island and never protected themselves sufficiently, even though warning signs were everywhere and the resort provided free sunblock in each room.

"I'll make sure she's taken care of," Drew said as he carefully tried to wake her. She partially opened her eyes, as if even that much took real effort.

"What's your full name?" Drew asked.

"Trinity Mathews," she said with a smile that lit up her face, causing his breath to quicken. He was trying to shake off the dizzying effect she was having on him, but nothing seemed to be working.

"Are you here with anyone?" As he asked, he found himself holding his breath. He'd noticed she wasn't wearing a ring, but that didn't mean anything.

"No, I'm on my own," she answered, then winced again. "My head really hurts."

"The doctor gave you a shot for that. It should kick in soon," he told her. She lay back down and drifted to sleep once more. Drew sent a staff member to get the information he needed on Trinity. She came back quickly and confirmed that Trinity was there alone and staying in one of the smaller rooms in the hotel. That was changing. Ms. Mathews had just earned an upgrade to his nicest suite.

He called a bellhop and had him go up ahead to have him move her things to the executive suite. He then had to wake her back up again.

"Trinity, the resort is moving you to a suite." She smiled as if she was only half listening, then closed her eyes again. Drew picked her back up, leaving the blanket around her before he trudged through the hotel. He didn't need to stare at temptation any longer, and he certainly didn't want other men looking.

They rode the elevator to the top floor. There were only a few rooms on that level and a special room key was needed to get up there. The bellhop held the suite door open so Drew could get Trinity inside without hitting her head again. He went straight for one of the large beds and laid her down.

She snuggled into the feather mattress and sighed. The doorman left and Drew found himself alone with the gorgeous female he couldn't quit fantasizing about. He woke again and she glared at him. He barely managed to suppress a smile. It was obvious she was getting tired of him waking her up.

"Trinity, I'm sorry to wake you, but the doctor said you need to get this lotion on or your skin will blister," he said. The pain medication the doctor had given her must have been working because her eyes closed again and she was out cold, completely ignoring his words.

Drew groaned as he realized he was going to have to apply the lotion. He looked skyward and wondered how much he could take if he had to touch her supple body. He sang out loud as he poured the lotion into his hands and began rubbing them together. The last thing he wanted to do, on top of everything else, was to shock her with cold lotion. OK, maybe he was trying to put off the inevitable.

Once the lotion seemed warm enough, he finally began applying it to her legs. He figured that starting with her legs would be easier on his libido. He was wrong, so very wrong. And by the time he'd finished smoothing the cream over her incredibly lush body, he had a throbbing erection and could barely breathe. Sweat was dripping off his brow.

Drew dashed from the room and jumped into an icy-cold shower. With grim determination, he stayed under the excruciating spray until his skin started turning blue and his goose bumps had their own goose bumps. Only then did he emerge. Once he could finally move his muscles again, he decided to grab his laptop and work. He couldn't leave Trinity alone, so he had a lot of time to kill.

He woke her every two hours at first. Each time, she'd give him a groggy answer before shutting her eyes again and falling back to sleep. The twenty-four hours couldn't end soon enough, because each time he saw her lying in the huge bed, he wanted nothing more than to climb in with her. He finally fell asleep in the middle of the night, exhaustion taking over from his long flight and tiring day.

CHAPTER THREE

AS TRINITY EMERGED slowly from a deep sleep, her only thought was *food*. She was starving, and her stomach rumbled loudly when she smelled a delicious aroma drifting toward her. As she turned over and opened her eyes, she realized she wasn't in her room. Before panic set in, she closed her eyes and concentrated. Had she gotten drunk and gone to a guy's room? That wasn't like her. No, no, her memory started to engage. It was a little hazy around the edges, but she could recall getting hit in the head.

One minute she was swimming, and the next thing she remembered was the sexiest guy she'd ever seen, leaning over her with panic-filled eyes. The details of his face eluded her, but she knew he'd been stunning enough to take her breath away, and that his eyes had been the same striking color as the sea behind him.

She vaguely recalled him carrying her, and that her head had been throbbing. Sleep had been a blessed relief because every time someone woke her up, she had to endure the pain.

Trinity lifted her hand to her head. She found a large lump

on the side, but her headache was gone. In fact, she felt pretty good — OK, her severely empty stomach wouldn't agree.

She climbed from the bed and looked in the closet; she was relieved to find her clothes there. Maybe she'd hit her head harder than she thought, and the hotel had moved her and she just couldn't remember. After slipping on a sundress, she followed her nose.

Trinity came to a standstill when she saw the man from the beach sitting at a table, removing lids from dishes of hot food. As she took in his features, more of her memory came streaming back, and she couldn't believe she'd forgotten a single thing about him, not his washboard abs or sexily defined arms —years in a coma couldn't make him forgettable.

Even after he looked up, then stood and pulled out a chair for her, she couldn't quit staring. She had to blink twice to make sure she really was seeing him. No mortal man was that... that...hell, she couldn't even think of an apt word to describe him. She shut her mouth quickly, afraid she'd ask him to remove his shirt so she could see if his torso was really as gorgeous as she remembered.

"How are you feeling, Trinity?" The sound of his voice startled her out of her deer-in-the-headlights moment.

"Fine," she responded automatically. When someone asked how you were, that's just how you answered. She never thought about how stupid that was before. She was in an unfamiliar room in a foreign land with a complete stranger, and she'd said she was fine. She really was anything but fine. It was even stranger that alarm bells weren't ringing. She'd heard of tourists being snatched by kidnappers or worse while in foreign lands, but she somehow didn't care.

Maybe she did have a head injury. After all, the knot *was* pretty big. But the only thing she could focus on was the food on the table.

"Are you hungry?" He asked her the one question she knew the answer to.

"Famished."

"Let's eat, then." He nodded to the chair he was holding out. Trinity's survival instincts finally seemed to kick in and she hesitated before moving closer to him.

"Where am I? Who are you? And why are we together?"

"You've been moved to one of our nicest executive suites. My name is Drew, and I've been looking after you because you were hit on the head and couldn't be by yourself."

His matter-of-fact answers reassured her enough to let her sit down. She knew she should ask more questions, but her stomach refused to shut up. He laughed at its growling, then quickly tried to cover the response with a very poor imitation of a cough.

"I'm sorry, but I don't remember when I ate last," she said as she grabbed a pancake, rolled it up and ate it plain, her favorite way. So what if pancakes weren't considered finger food. She didn't even have patience enough to spread butter and pour syrup. She wasn't sure why, but she couldn't remember ever being as hungry as she was at that moment. If this stranger happened to be stuffy and she offended him by breaking any rules of etiquette, it was his problem, not hers.

"I was actually getting ready to wake you up when you came out. You've been asleep for fourteen hours," he answered. No wonder she was so hungry. She'd gone straight to the beach the day before, without eating, then slept the entire rest of her day away.

"Why am I in the executive suite? There wasn't anything wrong with my room that I can remember."

"Because of your accident, the resort wanted to make your

stay a lot more comfortable," he answered. Trinity looked at him, finding his tone a little odd. He seemed nervous, which she couldn't understand. Yeah, he'd hit her, but he hadn't been aiming for her. Accidents happened.

"I've never actually stayed in a room this nice." Hey. This was exciting. Only he didn't seem to share the sentiment; he just looked around as if it wasn't anything new. Maybe he was used to luxury, but she wasn't, and she wouldn't let his lack of enthusiasm deflate her.

"I ordered a little of everything because I didn't know what you'd like."

Trinity was relieved when he broke the awkward silence. "Thank you. The pancakes are great. So, I guess I wasn't swimming in the right place, huh? I didn't even see any surfers out there when I got in the water."

"Waves were really bad yesterday, not ideal for surfing, so there were only a couple of tourists even trying. I was determined to find something, but then I hit you and..."

Trinity burst into laughter, cutting Drew off. When he stared at her as if she really did have a concussion and he should call the doctor, it caused her to laugh even harder.

"Sorry, really I am, but you have to admit it's pretty funny. I've never had a vacation before, ever, in my entire life. I'm always the good girl. It's an odd compulsion. I do everything — well almost everything — right and always plays it safe, and then on my first day of vacation, I take a swim and get whacked in the head. It's pretty amusing." She spoke between fits of laughter. Was the universe telling her to be afraid to take adventures? The heck with that. She wasn't letting anything ruin her very pricey vacation.

"I do feel bad about the accident, and I apologize."

"Seriously, it's not like you jumped in the water and thought to yourself, *hmm, I think I'd like to hit someone today,* so don't worry about it. After all, I did get this amazing suite and that's worth a nasty headache," she said. Trinity felt a bit of guilt over taking advantage of the situation. She really wasn't hurting. "I should tell them I'm not hurt so they aren't worried. As much as I love the room, I don't want to lie to get it."

"I'm sure they're more than happy to let you stay here and recuperate fully. Why not enjoy the nice room, which also just happens to have the most spectacular view on the entire island. Live it up and have a great vacation," he told her.

"I'm too tired to even think about moving at the moment, so I'll have to think some more on it. What time is it, anyway?" She asked.

"It's about five in the morning," he said with a yawn. "You slept the rest of the afternoon and most of the night."

"Wow, that's a bummer. I wasted an entire day of vacation. I'll just have to make up for it today," she said.

CHAPTER FOUR

DREW KNEW HE should just say goodbye and walk out the door. She was fine — she said so herself. She'd have a terrific vacation, on him, and never have to know. He couldn't seem to get his feet to move toward the door, though. He should run as fast as possible from the hotel, board his jet, and leave. He told himself he was going to do exactly that. He really intended to do just that, but somehow his tongue wouldn't listen to his brain.

"I'd love to be your tour guide," he offered. *No, no, no!* What was he thinking? He needed to get away from this woman, and now. She was causing his brain to be on permanent lock-down mode. To escort her all over the island would be madness.

"Are you here on vacation, too?" She asked.

"For now." Hey, that wasn't a lie exactly. He'd come for a vacation, hadn't he? OK, so it was only supposed to be for a few days, and it was his resort. That part he didn't want her to know. He didn't want to see the excited, almost innocent light leave her eyes, to be replaced by greed. And that *would* happen. He'd yet to meet a woman who wasn't affected by the amount of money he had. He should just stop this now — no lying, no disillusionment. But he knew there was no fighting himself. He had to get to know Trinity, just enough to ease his curiosity. His vacation just got extended.

"I'd love to have a tour guide," she said. Then she stopped speaking and looked at him with suspicion.

He raised his brow at her questioningly.

"What do you do for a living?" Trinity asked.

He knew it was a test of some sort, but he didn't know the right answer. He didn't want to tell her the truth, but he also didn't want to stray too far from the truth. Once anyone started weaving lies, breaking free from the web of deceit grew incredibly difficult.

"I work for the resort," he finally replied. It was the truth. Hell, he worked nonstop at his various resorts.

"Oh, you work here. But you said you're on vacation." The wrinkle returned to her forehead.

Danger signal!

Drew hastened to say, "I'm off for a few days, which is always a vacation when you're in paradise."

His answer seemed to be the right one because her face lit up and she went back to eating.

"In that case, I could most definitely use a guide, especially one who knows the area, but I don't want to take you away from your other activities," she said.

"Spending time with a beautiful lady is never a hardship." He gave her his most heart-stopping smile and stuck his hand out so they could shake on their deal. He'd been told by more than one woman that his smile stopped them in their tracks. He wasn't above using everything in his arsenal to seduce Ms. Trinity Mathews. Yes, that was his plan. It might be wrong of him, but he didn't care; the attraction was too strong, and he wanted her. And to judge by the way her eyes traveled along his body, she wanted him, too. She was just playing the game — she wanted to be chased and captured. He could feel it.

He watched Trinity hesitate before accepting his hand; was she afraid of touching him? Well, she should be afraid. He could practically taste the sulfur in the air from all the sparks that were flying. Finally, she stuck out her hand. Drew smiled when he saw goose bumps appear on her arm. Oh, yeah, he certainly affected her. So far, his vacation was turning out well.

Trinity pulled away from him and dashed into the bedroom without saying another word. He heard the shower start a few moments later and decided it was a good time to call his staff. He told them no one was to approach him with any business. He didn't care if the building was on fire. He was officially on vacation and didn't want his guest to know he was the boss.

Right after he hung up the phone, it rang again. Seeing that the caller was his main attorney, he answered reluctantly. Bad news. His attorney was faxing papers over and wanted to make sure Trinity signed them before the day was out. He was worried there'd be a huge lawsuit if she found out the person who had mowed her over in the water was the owner of the resort. Drew wanted to tell the guy to stick it, but he was a good lawyer, and a friend, one who had never steered him wrong, not in the ten years Drew had known him.

Drew called the resort manager and asked him to handle the paperwork. He made sure they were going to comp her room, all meals, and any activities she took part in for the rest of the week. Ms. Mathews had earned an all-inclusive free vacation. The attorney suggested a settlement of ten thousand dollars. Drew felt it was too small, but he'd see what her reaction was.

He prayed she didn't find out who he really was, because he had a feeling it really wouldn't go over well. In the meantime, he was going to give her the vacation of a lifetime.

When she returned from her shower, they headed downstairs.

"Ms. Mathews, can you step in here with me, please?" His manager approached them. Trinity looked at Drew with confusion. "I'm sorry, Ms. Mathews. I should have introduced myself. I'm Antony, the resort manager. I'd like to speak to you about yesterday and see if we can come up with a mutual agreement."

"Um, OK." Trinity nodded at him.

Drew stood and waited until she grabbed his hand. He hadn't wanted to go in with her, but he wasn't going to refuse her. He was curious about her reaction, though.

"We're very sorry about the incident yesterday. We take pride in having our guests thoroughly taken care of and satisfied with every aspect of their stay here. As you could see this morning, we've gone ahead and upgraded your room for the remainder of your time here. We've also credited back the payment for the week. All services at the hotel are on the house, and finally, we'd like to offer a settlement in the amount of ten thousand dollars. All you need to do is sign this paper and it's a done deal. If you need anyone to look over it, that's fine, as well. We don't want to rush you."

Drew watched her face the entire time his manger spoke. She seemed in shock, confused, and a little hopeful, but he didn't see open greed enter her eyes. He waited to see what she would say.

"I'll sign your papers, promising not to sue, but you really don't need to give me all this. I'm feeling a little guilty about it. It wasn't as if Drew went out there trying to hurt me, and apart from a small bump on my head, I'm fine. I don't even have a headache anymore." Sure, it would be nice to take the money and enjoy a free vacation, but it wasn't their fault that Drew ran into her. It wasn't even Drew's fault. It was just one of those freak accidents.

"Trinity, corporations make massive amounts of money and can afford a small settlement like this," Drew told her. "Besides, this is what insurance is for, right? Why don't you take what's being offered and have the vacation of a lifetime? Just think of all the spa services you can enjoy." Drew had a trust-me smile on his face.

"You really think so?" She asked and he nodded.

He waited anxiously as she turned back to the manager, who was nodding his encouragement while holding out the pen. She finally took it and signed the papers. Drew let out a relieved breath. He wanted to get her away from the office and start his seduction plans. He had a full day of romance planned.

"We're sorry your vacation has been interrupted, and hope this will help make up for it. Please take advantage of all our services and fully enjoy your stay," Antony said.

"Thank you; you've been very kind. Maybe I'll use the money to go to one of your other resorts," she said. She brightened up at the idea.

"That would be excellent, Ms. Mathews," Antony said. "If you decide to do that, give us a call and we'll make sure you get the royal service for a fraction of the cost."

Drew led her from the room and immediately steered her outside just as the sun was rising over the ocean. Even though it was early, it was still pleasantly warm, so the two of them sat in the sand to enjoy the view.

Drew pulled her in front of him and wrapped her in his arms. He felt her stiffen — was she struggling with the close contact? — but though he didn't let go, his grip was loose enough that she could pull away if she really wanted to. His heart pounded as he waited for her to decide what to do. Would she be open to a fling? Or, was it too much for her? This simple decision would effectively decide the rest of the vacation.

When she finally relaxed and laid her head against his chest, he had to fight the urge not to push her down on the sand and make love to her right then and there with the sun still rising over the ocean. Her presence alone was enough to send his body into overdrive, but touching her sent him over the top. He knew he'd never be able to look at a sunrise the same way again.

"What would you like to do next?" He whispered in her ear, making sure his breath caressed the sensitive skin. He was rewarded when a shiver racked her body. He rubbed his hand across her stomach, enjoying the feel of her quivering in his arms. He wanted to push further, but he knew she was skittish. If he pressed too hard, too fast, he'd walk away unsatisfied.

"I told you earlier, this is my first vacation, so I'm going to leave it up to you. Whatever you think would be fun and adventurous." She spoke in a mumble; her head was twisted against his shoulder and her eyes were shut.

What terrible temptation. There was only one fun and adventurous thing he wanted to do, and that involved them being in the bedroom — or anywhere they could comfortably lie down, or stand up, or… — day and night.

"OK," Drew told her, "but be prepared for the consequences of leaving it all to me." He had to quit playing the game he'd started, or he wouldn't be capable of walking anywhere without causing a major scene.

He slowly pulled his arms from around her, but he nearly gave in to his desire when he heard the barest whimper escape her lips. Trinity was just as turned on as he was. No, this wasn't the time for a quickie. Both of them deserved better. He'd spend the entire day building her body up, stoking her flames until she was ready to explode. By the time they did come together, the wait would be worth it. At least, that's what he told himself as he stood and then helped her to her feet.

He made sure their fingers were intertwine as they began walking down the beach. For once in Drew's life he wasn't in a hurry. He wanted her — that was always there, ever present in his mind, among other body parts. But, beyond wanting her, he enjoyed her. As they strolled along, speaking quietly, and getting to know each other, he found she was more than just a pretty face and spectacular body.

Whoa! He put the brakes on those thoughts and told himself to stick with the seduction plan, nothing more, even though he doubted it would be easy. Not with her.

CHAPTER FIVE

THE NEXT FEW days zipped by for Trinity. She was having the time of her life with Drew and didn't want her vacation ever to end. She'd invited him to use one of the spare rooms in her suite — she just didn't want him to leave. The old, cautious Trinity would never have done that. And she was having a hard time not asking him to share her bed. She couldn't be that bold, though. The only reason she was being brave was because she knew she'd never see him again after the week was over.

When they took a late swim in the heated pool, Trinity found herself more than a bit frustrated. She'd never in her life been so flirtatious with a man, and either he was completely clueless or he didn't desire her. Look, she had only two days left; it wouldn't hurt her to put herself out there. The worst that could happen? He'd refuse her.

Dang. A shudder went down her spine at the thought of such humiliation.

But to hell with it. Enough of being the good girl. Enough of caution. This vacation alone meant that she could change.

She was going to throw caution to the wind and just see what happened. If he still didn't make any moves, then she had her answer and could still call the vacation a success. She'd be sexually unsatisfied, but at least she'd still be relaxed.

"Mmm, this water is heavenly," she purred as she swam up close to him. Drew looked so unbelievably good in nothing but a pair of swim trunks. But as she swept up next to him, her stupid nerves started taking over. She'd never been the first person to initiate a kiss. The one time she'd tried to make the first move had been a few days ago, in another life, and that hadn't ended well.

As Trinity floated there, she was quickly losing her bravado. She wished she could be a femme fatale who could just barrel ahead and lock her lips to his, but she doubted she'd ever have that kind of courage.

She was now hanging onto the side of the wall, thinking it was time to get out of the pool, when he suddenly closed the last few inches between them and pressed their bodies close. She gulped in a quick breath of air as her breasts were crushed against his chest. She could feel heat instantly pool below her stomach, and her nipples hardened in anticipation of his touch. If he pulled back now, she'd lose all use of her body and sink to the bottom of the pool. She melted, and the man had done nothing more than press up against her.

Trinity felt utter joy as she watched Drew's eyes fill with desire. He growled low in his throat and pulled her even tighter against him. She couldn't miss the pressure of his obvious arousal against her, and she was desperate to have the few scraps of bathing suit material out of the way so he could plunge into her heat. Man, was she ready for him.

She watched in wonder as his eyes dilated a mere second before he lowered his head and brought their lips together in what became the most passionate kiss she'd ever received. His tongue traced her bottom lip before his teeth gently nipped it, causing her to open up to him. He thrust his tongue inside and caressed her mouth, demanding a response from her. She'd never been kissed so erotically, and her body quivered with excitement.

A deep moan escaped her throat as his tongue swept across her lips, across her tongue, and plunged in and out of her mouth. She lifted her arms so she could grip his hair and hold him in place. *Don't stop!* was her only thought. She shook as he rubbed his hands up and down her bare back. She was grateful that her tiny bikini didn't hide much of her skin from his hands, but it still wasn't enough. She wanted more. She wanted it all.

Trinity shivered as Drew ran his mouth down the smooth column of her throat and sucked the skin in at her pulse point, caressing her neck until she wanted to scream. He finally moved down to reach the vee between her breasts, making her breath hitch in anticipation.

She didn't realize they were moving until she felt the cool sensation of water rushing over her head as he pulled her underneath the waterfall at the end of the pool. They were suddenly enclosed in a cave, with the waterfall hiding them from any prying eyes.

Drew unlatched her bikini top and tossed it aside while he continued exploring her body. As his lips traced the top of her soft mounds, she couldn't stop groaning in pleasure. And when he latched on to her aching nipple, her back arched forward, and a guttural cry escaped her lips.

She felt the brush of his fingers on her hips as he untied her bikini bottom. She didn't even notice as it floated away to parts unknown.

She didn't care.

All she cared about was having her body joined with his. She needed him more than she needed air. From his passionate ministrations, she felt things exploding inside her that she'd never felt before. He brought his lips back to hers, and she grabbed hold of him like someone who was starving.

So this was the big deal about sex. She was finally starting to understand.

He pulled her legs up, and she eagerly wrapped them around his waist. She discovered to her surprise that he'd already discarded his khaki shorts and she felt his manhood press insistently against her core. She moved her hips forward to accommodate him — how she needed him inside her! He pushed forward and, with one deep thrust, buried himself inside her.

She cried out as he filled her. She was stretched further than ever before, and it took a moment for her body to adjust. He paused, but before she had time to catch her breath, he clasped her hips tightly, his fingers squeezing her rounded cheeks, and then he moved in and out of her moist heat. She threw her head back and cried out as the pressure started building to the point of no return. Drew traced her collar bone, suckling on her skin, as he moved faster within her.

In. Out. Over and over again, until she felt heat shoot from her core, through her limbs, and to every sensitive place on her body. Still, he didn't stop. He just continued moving, faster and faster until it was too much for her and she jerked in his arms. Her body tightened convulsively around his engorged staff as she flew over the edge in an explosion of pleasure.

As Trinity shattered from the inside out, she felt Drew tense. He pushed as far inside her as he could and cried out as he pumped deep within her womb. She felt him pulsing inside her core, and she loved that she'd brought him so much pleasure. If his feelings were anything like hers, he was a happy man.

Trinity couldn't even think about moving.

She stayed wrapped around Drew as her breathing started to return to normal. They were still connected intimately, and she didn't want to let go. After a few minutes, though, the water surrounding them made her start to shiver. And she finally started to think. Good grief! She was naked in a public pool! Thank heavens Drew had thought to pull them to the privacy of the cave, because until right then she hadn't been thinking of anything but her body's intense need.

"I don't know where my bathing suit went."

"I'm sorry about that," Drew said, but the huge smile splitting his face didn't seem very apologetic.

Trinity saw the humor in the situation and started to giggle. If only her friends could see her now, they certainly wouldn't recognize her.

"Hey, who's in there?" They heard someone calling. Her laughter instantly stopped and she was mortified someone knew she was in the secluded cave, and worse than that, most likely knew what she was doing. She began to look around with real panic. She spotted her top and put it on, but couldn't find the bikini bottom.

"I'll go find them. Wait here," Drew said, still sporting the same grin. She huffed out an indignant breath. As if she had any other choice but to wait. She wasn't going out there half naked — the most embarrassing half, too. He quickly disappeared while she huddled in the privacy of the cave, shivering with cold. She heard Drew speaking with whoever was out there, but couldn't hear what they were saying.

He came back through the waterfall a few minutes later and she was incredibly grateful to see the bottom part of her swimsuit in his hands. He handed it over and she struggled to put it back on under the water.

"I knew the guard on duty, and he's gone now. Let's sneak out of here and go back to the room," he whispered once she finally had her suit situated. She nodded and followed him out of the cave. She looked around nervously, very happy that no one else was around. She climbed from the pool, quickly wrapping a towel around her shaking body.

Drew grabbed her hand and they headed through the back hallways and stepped onto an elevator. Trinity didn't breathe fully until they were safely inside the luxurious suite.

"I can't believe I did that," she said as she stared up at the man who'd just shifted her entire universe. She was shocked to realize she didn't feel any guilt over what she'd done. It had been amazing, and she'd carry the memory with her on those long, cold, rainy nights back home.

"Believe it or not, I've never before been so hungry for a woman that I lost my head like that," Drew said with a look of disbelief on his face.

Trinity was gratified to learn that he didn't do that with all the tourists. She knew it was just a vacation fling, but still, every woman wanted to feel special.

"I'm going to take a shower. I'm freezing and can't quit shaking," she told him and headed to the bathroom.

"I'll join you, to save on water," he said with a waggle of his brows.

Why not? She'd already leaped before she looked, so why not enjoy her last two days in paradise to the fullest? She nodded her head, and he scooped her into his arms as he stepped into the shower stall.

His caveman tactic had made her giggle, but not for long. They made love again, and again in the water, but this time the spray was cascading over them, and it was warm. Trinity suspected that she'd be unable to see water again without quivering with need.

They crawled from the shower and straight into bed. Drew pulled her into his arms, caressing her back, which made her want to purr. She told herself to be careful, because she could feel her heart starting to swell. *It's just a fling, only a fling*, she repeated over and over to herself. She wouldn't become another cliché and fall for the rebound guy.

Trinity almost convinced herself she could do it without her heart getting involved. But as she fell asleep a smile of pure happiness sat on her lips, and her dreams would be filled with him. He wasn't a forgettable kind of man.

CHAPTER SIX

DREW FELT MORE relaxed than he had in too long to remember, and thought he could lie next to her until the end of eternity. He doubted he'd be able to let her go in two days. He tried to say the words aloud, but didn't know where to start. If she found out who he really was, she was going to be angry, but they couldn't possibly continue to see each other under false pretenses.

He didn't understand how he'd gotten himself into such a bad position. He needed to figure out how to fix it. Hell, he built billion-dollar resorts that were visited by royalty, so he could certainly figure out how to work out a relationship with one small woman, couldn't he?

He fell asleep, still struggling with what to do. But he reassured himself with the thought that he had a couple of days left. He'd done far more difficult things with far less time.

* * *

Trinity stepped out of the elevator with Drew by her side.

It was her last day in paradise and she had to keep reminding herself that her time with him was special because it was short. Much as she didn't want to admit it, her impulsive behavior had rattled her a little. But she was determined to convince herself that this was a great vacation, a short affair, and nothing more. Why was her mind giving her such trouble?

It was taking everything in her not to ask for his number. She couldn't call him once she left, or she'd just be one of those females who went straight from one relationship to another. Besides, long-distance relationships never worked, and there was no way she could afford to fly back, not even once a year.

"Where do you live in the States?" Drew asked her as they entered the restaurant for breakfast.

Trinity laughed. "If I tell you, then the magic of our time together starts to fade."

"I make it there sometimes and would love to come see you," he said.

"I don't think it's a good idea. This has been unbelievable, but if we try to stay in contact, the real world will break in." She spoke so quietly that she she could hardly hear herself over the thumping of her heart. She wanted so badly to say to hell with caution and just go for it.

"You don't have to tell me exactly where you live; just name a state. If it's meant to be, we'll run into each other at a romantic little café on a rainy day. That will be the moment we realize we can't stand to be apart and are meant to be together," he said with a wicked smile.

She knew, of course, that even if she told him the state, the likelihood that he'd actually find her was slim to none.

"I live in rainy Washington," she finally said.

He seemed to tense for a moment and then relaxed and plastered his easy smile back on. She had most likely imagined the moment. Drew never seemed to get stressed.

CHAPTER SEVEN

DREW COULDN'T BELIEVE his luck. She actually lived in Washington. Here was the most perfect woman he'd ever met and she lived in the same state he did. What were the odds he'd meet her in another country? He traveled a lot, but mostly by choice now. His resorts were running well without his constant on-site supervision. He had no new projects in the works, and he was spending a lot more time at home with his cousins. With Derek married, they all seemed to revolve around him, his wife, Jasmine, and their kids.

Granted, he wasn't altogether happy to be so hung up on Trinity, especially after knowing her for only about a week, but he couldn't imagine never seeing her again. Normally, he never deviated from a plan, and she was supposed to be nothing more than a stress-relieving fling. She was much more than that, though. The thought of saying goodbye was too painful to even think about.

"I'm in the beautiful Northwest often," he finally told her, and he focused on her face, needing to know whether he was wasting his time. Yes! He saw the small bit of hope his words caused to flare up, though she tried to hide it.

She was just as affected as he was, and he was going to fight for the chance to make her his, at least until he could figure out why she had such power over him, why she was stirring so many confusing emotions.

* * *

Trinity hated the way her heartbeat sped up at his words. She didn't want him to give her hope of seeing him again. It would make those long winter nights even longer. Face it. She was starting to fall a little too hard for this enigmatic man. They never should have started talking about life outside the resort — she knew that. *Keep it casual.* The only way not to get hurt was to refuse to let it grow at all serious.

"I'm going to be honest, Drew, even though it's really hard for me to express myself. I'm always the pushover. My last boyfriend, whom I thought I was going to eventually marry, decided to bed his secretary, and that's why I'm on this very impulsive vacation. I'm grateful I took it, and even more grateful I met you. I regret nothing that's happened, but if I keep in contact with you when I get back to the real world, it'll change how I feel. I'll start thinking of happily ever after, instead of right now, and I'm not the girl you think I am. You won't like me when I'm back in the real world." A tear escaped.

"I could never dislike you, Trinity, no matter where we are. Take my phone number, and I'll wait each day for the call to come in. If you can trust me, even a little bit, you could offer me yours." He held a piece of paper out to her.

Trinity stared at that piece of paper, and she wanted to take so badly. What would it really hurt if she took it? She didn't have to call if she didn't want to. She could even throw it away at the airport. It didn't change anything if she just slipped it in her pocket. She could throw it away later. But if she didn't have it and she found herself really wanting to talk to him, there'd be no way to find him again. If she gave him her number and he never called, she could just look at this as a magical dream. But then, if he did call, maybe, just maybe, they could have a nice night together at some point in the future. Probably not. It was just an island romance, and she'd be fine once she got home… But just in case. She reached out and took the slip of paper, and she watched his face practically glow as he rewarded her with a smile.

"OK, we'll do it your way," she said with a hesitant smile, "but believe me, I'll be the first to say I told you so when you realize how boring I am."

"Let me be the judge of that, Trinity." He leaned down and gave her a heart-stopping kiss. "Where's your number for me?"

"I'll write it down in our room. You know, this has been the best vacation I've ever had, even if it's the only one, too." This time, her smile was wide.

"How about we make it a few extra days?" he asked.

And he did look completely serious. A few extra days couldn't hurt, could they? Her cautious brain was screaming, "Run away," but she told it to shut up.

"I might be able to do that." When she uttered the words, his smile was so brilliant, it was almost blinding. She knew it was a real risk to her heart to stay longer, but she couldn't seem to listen to her brain. She was enjoying her time with Drew, and she refused to feel guilty about it, to worry about consequences.

"Let's go tell the hotel you're keeping that room a little while longer," he said, and he grabbed her arm.

"I can go back to my original room. They aren't going to want me to stay in the suite," she said with a laugh at his enthusiasm. "I need to make sure I can change my tickets, as well," she finished, trying to sound reasonable.

"Remember, you're being impulsive, so don't worry about any of it," he said, as they got closer to the front desk.

"Drew, is that you?" Trinity felt Drew's body tense at the greeting. She turned to see who would make him so nervous. She figured it had to be a former lover, but she knew he hadn't been a monk before her. She wanted to reassure him that she didn't care about a past fling.

"Hello, Nancy. How are you?"

The woman Drew was speaking to had to be in her late forties, at least. Trinity really didn't see why he was so nervous around her. Maybe she'd hit on him or something at some point, and he was uncomfortable, or maybe he was embarrassed that he'd had a relationship with an obviously wealthy older woman, but he couldn't be impolite because he worked at the resort.

Trinity hadn't even thought about Drew's job. She'd been there a week and he hadn't gone to work once. That seemed strange. She'd need to ask him about that after the woman left.

"I'm just wonderful. You have a beautiful resort here, and I'm so glad we decided to stay," she said with a soft laugh of delight. "I've just finished with your amazing spa and feel like I'm floating on a cloud."

"I'm happy you're enjoying yourself. We're in a hurry, but I'd love to chat with you later," he said, and then he spun Trinity around as if he couldn't get out of there fast enough. Trinity had to jog a bit to keep up with him.

* * *

As they neared the doors, Drew wanted nothing more than to make it outside. He'd just had a very close call. He'd avoid the lobby for the next few days. The last thing he needed right now was for Trinity to find out who he really was. Not yet, not until he'd spent more time with her. He'd never felt this way with any other woman. He would come clean with her, but he'd have to do it at the right moment, and the right moment certainly wasn't in the middle of his damned lobby.

"Drew, I'm sorry to bug you again, but my husband really wanted to meet you and talk about the golf course." The woman he'd just escaped had followed him out, and Drew knew he was probably in for it. "Darling, this is Drew Titan, the owner of the resort. Drew, my husband, Dean."

Drew shook the man's hand and sighed as he felt Trinity pull away from him. He had never been terrified to face anything before, but he sure as hell didn't want to turn and see the expression on her face.

When the couple walked away, he finally faced her.

She was staring at him as if he'd just run over her puppy. As a single tear slipped from her eye, he reached up to try to comfort her. If she'd only let him explain, he knew he could make everything better. Suddenly, her hand shot out and she slapped him hard enough across the face that it echoed through the lobby.

Several heads turned to stare at them. The security guard started walking forward, but Drew shook his head. He deserved that one, he figured.

"Let me explain…"

"Don't waste your time, Mr. Titan. I don't know why you even bothered with the entire seduction scene, considering I signed those papers pretty quickly for you. Is there something else you need me to sign to assure you that your precious resort is safe from my greedy clutches?"

"I'm not worried you'll sue the resort," he almost shouted.

The entire scene was quickly getting out of hand. "I just wanted a week with a beautiful woman who didn't know who I was. That doesn't make me the bad guy you think I am."

"Oh, I'd never say you were a bad guy. You did everything perfectly. You wined and dined me. You swept me off of my feet. You were an absolutely perfect host, and I never want to see you again," she snarled, and then walked away.

Drew watched as she left the room with her back straight and her head pointed forward. She didn't turn around once, didn't give him one last look.

OK. He'd give her a little time to cool off, and then they could talk. Once her anger abated, she'd realize he wasn't the villain in this story. They'd gotten to know each other pretty well in the past days, and she'd have to see that he wasn't what she'd accused him of. But even though it wasn't noon yet, he ordered a double scotch and sat with his head in his hands.

So he gave her what he thought was enough time to herself, then made his way back up to the suite. He stood there in shock. She was gone. The only item she'd left behind was the single slip of paper with his number on it. Other than that, the only evidence that she even existed was the slight scent of peach drifting in the air that he knew he'd forever associate with her. He walked back out of the room, knowing he'd never sleep in there again.

CHAPTER EIGHT

Five months later

TRINITY STRUGGLED TO get to her feet, which was becoming harder with each passing day. Her back was hurting particularly badly, and she was feeling far grumpier than usual.

"Excuse me, is anyone here?" Trinity wasn't entirely happy to have a new customer. She owned a fairly successful floral shop, but some days she wished it were a bit less busy.

When she'd found out she was pregnant, she'd panicked at first. The more time she had to think about it, though, the more excited she became. She was now eager to hold her little girl in her arms. She'd received her first photos of her unborn daughter only a few weeks ago, and she'd been far too pumped up to wait to find out the baby's gender. Besides, she was on a tight budget and had to search for clothing when it was on sale.

Drew had tried calling her for the first month after she got home, but he'd finally taken the hint that she didn't want to talk to him, and he'd left her alone ever since. She didn't even want to think about how he'd gotten her phone number. She'd found out she was pregnant a couple weeks after his last call, but she wasn't ready to talk to him about it yet. Yes, she knew she'd have to tell him eventually, but she wasn't looking forward to the conversation. She just wanted to bask in the glow of her pregnancy for as long as she could — swollen ankles and all.

She sure as heck wasn't basking in any glow that afternoon. Not only was her back killing her, but her feet were at least twice their normal size, and she'd been busy all afternoon. Thank heavens the day was almost over.

"Sorry about that; it's taking me a little longer to get to my feet these days," Trinity said, as she finally got up.

The woman smiled as if she understood.

"Is this your and your husband's first child?"

"This is my first child. I'm not married, though." Trinity didn't know why she felt the need to give such personal details.

"Oh," the woman said in a tight voice. She was almost sneering. "I don't really need anything after all." She turned to walk out the door.

Trinity was in shock. What century was she in that someone would look down on her because she was pregnant and not married? She decided to close a few minutes early; her day wasn't going to get any better. She walked to the glass door and turned the sign, then saw a familiar face through the glass panel.

"Hello, beautiful," said her best friend, Damien Whitfield.

"You're a breath of fresh air, Damien. It's been a rough day," Trinity replied as he flung his arms around her for a hug.

"I always like to hear that from a beautiful lady," he said with his normal good humor. "I'm taking you out for a terrific dinner and the new horror flick."

"That sounds heavenly." She needed to watch some zombies eating their way through the human race. It would help take her mind off her worries, especially that last customer. After locking up, she followed him to his vehicle and they were soon off.

They'd been best friends since high school and were always there for each other. Any time one of them went through a bad breakup, the other could be counted on to bring ice cream and a horror flick. She didn't know how she could make it through the pregnancy if Damien weren't around.

"I've been trying to work up the courage to speak to you about something, but haven't known how to approach it," he said as they finished eating dessert.

"You know you can talk to me about anything, Damien." She beamed at him.

"OK, I'm just going to go for it, Trinity. I want you to really listen to me and seriously think about what I'm saying."

His tone of voice worried her, so she reached across the table and took his hand encouragingly in hers.

"I think we should get married — no, wait, don't start shaking your head yet. Remember, you promised to listen."

"OK, I'll listen, but you're crazy," she just had to say.

"It's really not that crazy, if you think about it. We're best friends and truly love each other. We've always been there for each other. Plus, we never fight. Neither one of us has been able to find the right person, and now you have this baby girl coming in four short months, and just in case that isn't enough, I'd make a terrific father." Damien said it all in one breath.

"But Damien, we've never been more than friends. There has to be more than just friendship." She hoped he'd see reason. She didn't feel any physical attraction toward her best friend, though he was stunningly handsome. She knew women threw themselves at him all the time, but she'd been in friend zone with him too long. But she could hardly say that to him, though. There was no reason to be hurtful.

"I'm simply asking you to think about it. I can take care of you and the baby, and I think we could be happy," he said, all the while staring into her eyes.

Trinity did love Damien and loved that he was trying to help. She wished she loved him romantically, because he was about the most perfect guy she'd ever known. But he simply didn't make her stomach quiver the way Drew had. She shook her head to push that thought from her mind. Drew wasn't a factor in any of her decisions.

The baby kicked her just as she had that last thought, and Trinity had to smile. Her little girl was a huge reminder that Drew was a factor, and would be one for the rest of her life. But she couldn't think about that right then. He'd lied to her, making him no better than her cheating ex. She couldn't possibly trust him to be a part of her life.

She forced her mind back to Damien's proposal. "Let me think about things, Damien."

"Take your time, Trinity. I know it's a huge decision, but I really do mean it. I'll take care of you, and love every second of doing it."

"What happens if you meet the one and you're stuck with me?" She asked.

He responded with his own question. "What if you're the one, but we never realized it?"

She laughed and promised to let him know soon. They went to their movie, and the rest of the evening was as relaxed as it always was. She had a feeling both of them would regret it if she said yes, but it was tempting.

He pulled up in front of her apartment and walked her to her door, just as he always did. They had never had one of those classic awkward moments before, but they certainly were having one now. He took a deep breath and bent down to kiss her goodnight.

Trinity's first instinct was to pull away and ask him what he could possibly be thinking, but the man had proposed marriage, so it stood to reason he'd want to share a kiss. She made herself relax as he brushed his tongue across her lips. His arms wrapped around her awkwardly, and she laid her own hands on his arms as he drew out the kiss.

She just wanted it to end.

It saddened her to no end to realize that she felt absolutely nothing. There was no spark, no heat, no light-headedness, no crazy chemistry — nothing, just a void. She wasn't repulsed, but it was like kissing her cousin. He finally pulled away, and she saw the regret in his own eyes. It was obvious he'd felt nothing, as well.

"I'll leave you for now. Let me know what you decide. Our marriage doesn't have to be about passion. It can be about friendship and loving your baby girl," he said.

She wasn't sure whether he was trying to convince her or himself. It didn't really matter, she thought, because it wasn't about either of them. It was about her baby.

She reached up on her toes and kissed him softly on the cheek, then went through her door. She leaned against it as a single tear fell down her cheek. If only she'd felt at least a smidgen of passion from her best friend. Then she could say yes without guilt. It would be nice to have someone to share her life with. Sometimes, she was just so lonely.

As Trinity climbed into bed that night, she replayed her week in paradise, the way she did most nights. She'd yet to wake without at least one dream of Drew lingering on her consciousness. How could a man she'd known for such a short amount of time still have a lasting effect on her? She fell asleep with tears now flowing freely — another of her nightly rituals.

CHAPTER NINE

YOU CAN'T KEEP a good girl down, Trinity told herself, even when the good girl wasn't that good anymore. At least some of the swelling had gone down, so she felt a bit more human. And she was closing up shop for the night — at last! She'd been struggling with Damien's proposal for a week now, and she'd finally decided to accept. It was time to be realistic. She'd tried and failed with romance; why not try friendship as the basis for a lasting relationship? They were close, as close as any two people could get. If they could just avoid the whole sex thing, she'd be fine. And it would be nice to have him there to help raise her child.

The two of them had spoken several times on the phone since their awkward kiss, and everything was fine. They didn't discuss the lack of passion, but focused on their friendship, as they always had. She was lucky to have such a wonderful man she could turn to.

It was far more important to have security and love than to have passion. She'd loved Damien for a long time, and she was sure it could grow if she wished for it. She'd just demand that her body respond to him. She was stubborn enough; surely she could will her body to obey.

She watched Damien walk toward the shop as soon as she was finished locking the door. With a deep breath, she got ready to tell him her decision. He seemed to know she was ready to talk to him, because he said nothing as he approached. He just waited for her to gather her thoughts. She finally looked into his beautiful green eyes. He really was attractive. That she didn't desire him made no sense at all.

"Damien, I'll marry you" she said with a tentative smile. "That is, if the offer's still on the table."

"That's wonderful, Trinity!" Damien wrapped his arms around her expanding body and kissed her forehead.

She felt as if she were at home when she was in his arms. It had to be the right decision. Doubts? What doubts? She refused to acknowledge them. She also refused to acknowledge that his hug did nothing more than comfort her.

"I think we should do it before the baby is born," he told her. "If you want a big wedding, that's fine. It's all up to you. I want your wedding day to be special, and you know money isn't an issue. We'll have a good marriage, and I don't want you to have regrets about the wedding itself."

"No, we can do it at the courthouse. I don't have anyone I'd invite to a real wedding anyway," she said a bit sadly.

They started down the street together toward her apartment, which wasn't far away. Their hands joined together as they made their way along the sidewalk. That was a natural thing — they were comfortable touching one another. Heck, she'd fallen asleep in his arms before while on the couch watching movies. They were relaxed with each other; that was why their friendship worked.

"I didn't even think about getting you a ring. I'll do that

tomorrow," he said as they climbed the stairs and turned the corner.

She hadn't thought about a ring either. Face it — she didn't really think of the marriage as real. She had to fight back tears, because she knew she was settling, and what was even worse, she was making him do so as well.

"I don't need a fancy ring, Damien, just a simple band," she told him right before they turned the corner onto her hall.

"What do you need a ring for?" she heard Drew ask.

Trinity stopped suddenly and looked into the deep blue eyes she hadn't seen in five months. The air started spinning for a moment, and she felt panic start deep inside her gut. She hadn't expected to see him again and certainly not in this situation. And despite everything that had happened, an unbelievable rush of attraction washed over her from just the sight of him standing there. Oh, why couldn't she feel the same way with Damien?

"What are you doing here?" She was barely able to whisper.

"I asked you a question first," Drew said as he glared from her to Damien, and then down to her stomach. He had thought of no other woman but her over the last five months and he wasn't happy to find her with another man. Hell, not only that, but she was clearly pregnant. By the looks of her stomach, the child was either his or she'd jumped into the arms of another guy immediately following their affair. Either way, he definitely wasn't happy with her at that moment.

She could see he was trying to figure out exactly how far along she was. She heard a door open across the hall. That was all she needed. She had to get away from her nosy neighbor before having this incredibly personal conversation.

"I'm tired, Drew, and don't want to talk right now. My shop, which is right down the street, will be open tomorrow. Why don't you come over around noon?" She opened her door and stepped inside. Damien followed behind her slowly, and Drew was right on his heels. She glared at him as he entered her sanctuary uninvited and looked around.

"I think we'll talk now, and I'd still like to hear why you need a ring," Drew said firmly.

Trinity couldn't believe she'd ever thought the man was simply a resort employee. He exuded raw power, in both manner and dress. And to her horror, her traitorous body responded to him. He was even more impressive than she remembered, if that were possible.

"We're getting married," Damien said, since it was obvious she wasn't going to say anything.

Trinity was both annoyed and grateful that Damien had stepped up and said something. She was too emotional to think, much less speak.

"I see it didn't take you long to bounce back after our relationship, or is this the man who cheated on you?" Drew sneered.

"None of it is any of your business, Drew. You need to leave, now. We have nothing else to talk about."

He looked at her rounded stomach again, then back to her face, and she could feel the heat redden her cheeks. His eyes grew even narrower, and Trinity had to fight not to flinch.

* * *

"How far along are you, Trinity?" Drew hadn't forgotten that they hadn't used protection their first time in the pool. He wasn't the kind of guy who had unprotected sex; he just wasn't so stupid. But he'd lost his mind a lot that week. He'd assumed that she'd contact him if there were consequences from their week. Hell, for that matter, he'd tried calling her for a month straight. He wasn't used to being rejected and her rejection had wounded his pride — more so than he'd ever admit.

He'd figured that her anger would have cooled off after five months. And because he couldn't get his mind off her, he finally decided he had to see her again. OK, so he owned the stupid resort. She'd just have to get over it. And if she found out he owned a whole passel of resorts? He wasn't looking forward to that, She'd most likely never speak to him again, whether the child was his or not.

Still, Drew wasn't backing down. He needed to know whether the child she carried was his. He refused to take his eyes from her, and she finally let out a heavy sigh.

"I'm five months," she said with her head held high.

Drew blew out his breath. Though she didn't try to lie, she obviously didn't want him to know. Why didn't she? She had to have figured out by now that he was a wealthy man. From the looks of her apartment, she'd need financial help to raise the baby. But first things first.

"The baby is mine, then."

"It doesn't matter, Drew. We had a week together and it didn't work out. I don't expect anything from you, so you're free to leave. I know how you like your papers signed, though. If you have your attorney fax them to my shop, I'll sign whatever you need to be released from responsibility, and you can be on your merry way."

Each word that Trinity spoke angered Drew further. She didn't let it sink in that he was going to be a father. Half a second after giving him the news, she was telling him he wasn't needed. How dare she try to discard him, not once, but twice? He'd never walk away from his child. She'd soon be in no doubt of that.

As quickly as his temper flared, it receded when he saw her sink wearily to the couch as if she couldn't remain on her feet for even a moment longer. His instinct was to go to her, offer comfort. But not. He held himself back, though with difficulty. He needed to hold on to his anger. He began pacing the tiny apartment, barely able to take three steps before having to turn around.

* * *

"Trinity, you need to figure all of this out," Damien said, "so I'm going to leave. Call me if you need me and I'll be here within a few minutes." After glaring at Drew, he walked out of the apartment, leaving her alone with the man who'd changed her life forever.

Trinity didn't want Damien to go, but it wasn't fair for her to make him stay and deal with her problems. She watched as he walked out the door and then she let out the breath she didn't know she was holding.

Drew continued pacing her apartment — almost stomping backward and forward — and it was obvious that he was furious. When he finally turned to face her, she almost recoiled. At least her pregnancy had one upside: it made her feel a little safer. He wasn't the sort to do a woman bodily harm, but he looked as if he wanted to. She'd never seen a man so pissed off before.

"Were you going to tell me about the baby, Trinity?"

She didn't think he'd like her answer, so it took a moment, and she still stumbled over the words.

"I would have… eventually." She didn't see how it mattered either way. They weren't a couple, after all. She'd have thought he'd rejoice that she wasn't asking him for anything. Didn't most men run in the other direction when women so much as mentioned marriage or babies?

"Who was that guy?" Drew couldn't help but ask.

"That's Damien. We decided to get married," she said in a matter-of-fact tone. She was so exhausted, she couldn't even think, much less be careful about what she was saying, or who she was saying it to.

"How long have you been seeing him?"

"He's my best friend." When she thought about her conversation with Drew later, she'd realize that she should have tried to sound more like a woman in love. But she and Damien had never been more than friends, and to pretend that they were a romantic pair was almost impossible.

"Why are you marrying him?" Drew asked more calmly, and because she still wasn't thinking properly, she answered honestly.

"He wants to help me with the baby," she said simply.

If she had looked up and seen his face, she would have realized her mistake.

"You want another man to raise my child?"

The tone of his voice made her look up, and what she saw took her breath away. She could understand now how he was the businessman he was. The look of pure fury in his eyes was enough to make a strong man quiver at his feet. Trinity knew that a quick retreat was the only safe option.

"Look, we both know the week we had was a mistake," she finally said. "I'm not going to punish my child by trying to pretend otherwise." Her braveness amazed her. Pregnancy had done wonders for her confidence…and temper.

"Tell your friend the marriage is off, because the real father will be doing the right thing," he growled.

Her temper shot up another notch. She was close to

matching him in the who's-scarier contest.

"Don't be ridiculous, Drew."

"I'm the one being ridiculous? You were trying to keep my child from me, and I'm being ridiculous? If I hadn't shown up here, you never would have told me," he practically shouted.

"I'm exhausted, and I'm done with this conversation." Trinity stood up and headed out of the room. "Please lock the door behind you." She sat on the edge of her bed and shook as she waited to hear the sound of the lock clicking on her door. She was afraid he'd follow her. She wasn't afraid he'd physically harm her; the real fear was that he'd touch her.

Even as she was ready to throw a punch at him, she still couldn't stop the desire burning just below the surface. Five months away from the man, and the second she saw him standing there, she'd wanted to rip his clothes off.

Trinity waited for the sound of the door latching before she collapsed on her bed. As her emotions simmered down, she was filled with a bone-weary exhaustion. She wanted nothing more than a full night's rest, and to wake up to find it had all been nothing but a bad dream.

CHAPTER TEN

DREW WAS LEFT speechless. She'd actually walked away. And that never happened — people just didn't defy him. Certainly no one ever dismissed him the way Trinity just had. It was only when he heard the click of her bedroom door that he thought of going after her.

Should he break her door down and demand that they finish the conversation? No, exhaustion had been written all over her face, and he was sure that wasn't good for his son or daughter. As Drew took in his surroundings, a sense of claustrophobia began to set in. How did she think she could raise their child in such a small space? He couldn't find a single spot available for a crib, let alone all the other items needed for a baby.

His cousin had one tiny infant, and one preteen, and their house was strewn with their toys and other debris. Not even a percentage of that stuff would fit in her small space. He had to admit that she kept it clean and inviting — well, as inviting as a box could be.

Drew sank down onto her couch as reality started to really set in. He was going to have a child in four short months. He wasn't prepared for it, but then again, who was ever prepared?

He glanced at her coffee table, where several bills lay scattered among paperwork. He noticed the words *three-dimensional sonogram,* and he straightened up. He quickly scanned the paper, and his hand stilled as he read the words telling him he was going to have a daughter. A tiny baby girl would be in his arms in only four short months.

When Drew moved to set the paperwork back down, a small picture fluttered to the floor, face up. He stared at it for several moments before reaching out and gently grasping the corner, afraid to hurt the image. He couldn't even breathe as he took in the glorious sight of his daughter's first picture.

He felt his smile spread as he looked at her. It looked to him as if she even had his Titan nose. She was the most beautiful girl he'd ever seen. Unfamiliar emotions overtook him. He finally released the photo and stood up. He could hardly breathe.

Drew made a beeline for her front door, making sure it was securely locked behind him, then headed down the staircase.

When he stepped outside, he found Damien leaning against a wall, obviously waiting for him. As the fresh air cleared Drew's befuddled brain, he almost hoped Trinity's friend wanted a fight. He could really use a target to take some of his aggression out on.

The two men stood only a couple of feet apart, and neither lowered their hardened gazes from the other. Drew had to give the guy grudging respect that he was willing to stand up for his friend. However, Damien needed to realize that he was messing with Drew's woman and child. That was a no-go.

Drew finally broke the silence. "I'll be marrying Trinity."

"I figured as much," Damien said with a cocky smile.

Drew relaxed when he realized Damien wasn't planning to fight for her.

"Why are you still hanging around, then?" Drew asked.

"I wanted to make sure Trinity was going to be OK. She's been my best friend for a lot of years. We've always taken care of each other, which is why I offered to marry her in the first place. I don't want her to be alone," Damien replied.

"I can understand that. I would have done the same thing."

"Just know, if you hurt her, you'll have to answer to me." Damien stood to his full six-foot-plus height.

Drew didn't back down, but he acknowledged that the man was doing no more than he'd do for someone he loved. He finally nodded his head, which seemed to satisfy Damien. He'd done what he felt was right, and he could relax now.

"Let's get a drink," Drew said. He wanted to learn more about Trinity's Damien, a fellow who was so willing to become an instant father to another man's child. He also wanted to know what Trinity had been up to the last five months.

"I could use a beer," Damien replied, the tension evaporating as quickly as it has come. The men walked down the street in a comfortable silence.

"How's she been?" Drew asked as they sat down in a sparsely populated bar.

"She's been depressed ever since she got back from her vacation. I knew something was up, but at first, I assumed she was still upset over her breakup with her ex-boyfriend. Soon, though, it was obvious something else was going on. She didn't tell me about the pregnancy until she could no longer hide it. It was the first time she'd ever kept something from me — which sent up red flags. She wouldn't talk about you. Not a single word… What the hell did you do to her?"

Drew sighed and decided he might as well tell the story to her best friend. He figured the guy just might end up being his ally in the whole mess.

Drew gave Damien a shortened version, and when he finished speaking, Damien sat back with a slight chuckle.

"Glad I'm not in your shoes," Damien finally managed to say.

"Yeah, thanks for that." Though they were both getting in some cheap shots at each other, Drew felt comfortable around the fellow. He appreciated that Damien had stepped up and been there for Trinity when she'd needed him most. As much as he hated to admit it, he found himself actually liking her best friend.

"Just calling it how I see it," Damien said.

After his own confession, and Damien's filling him in on the last five months of Trinity's life, Drew started to relax. He was back in the States, he'd found the girl he hadn't been able to stop thinking about, and he was going to be a father. He knew he had to speak with Derek. It wouldn't feel completely real until he shared the news.

He ended his evening with Damien, with the two of them exchanging phone numbers in case anything came up with Trinity, and then he jumped into his vehicle and took the shortest route he could to Derek's house.

His fingers were shaking so badly that he had to re-enter the code to open the gate three times. Then, in his wild impatience, it seemed to take forever to make his way up the long driveway. But as the huge house came into view, he felt most of his stress fade away. Derek would have the rest of the answers Drew was searching for. The problem was, he didn't know what he wanted to hear.

He just needed…hell, he didn't know.

The minute Drew walked through the front doors, it was like coming home. He was drawn to the back of the house by the sound of laughter; everyone was clearly hanging out by the pool. Inner turmoil be damned! He couldn't help but smile as he stepped through the patio doors and spotted his cousin Derek and his son, Jacob, in the middle of a splashing war.

Jacob looked up and gave him a huge grin. "Uncle Drew, you're back," the boy yelled as he jumped from the pool to give him a very wet hug.

Drew loved every second of it.

"How are you doing, squirt?"

"I'm good. I was totally crushing my dad." Jacob was bouncing on his feet. He was full of energy all day long — then he crashed hard.

Derek walked up next to his son. "Hey, I was just waiting to make my big comeback." He shook Drew's hand, then raised his eyebrows. "You're back in town early." The cousins knew each other well, and Derek could see something was wrong.

"Hey, buddy, can you let your mom know Drew's here, and see if she can make us something to eat?" Derek asked Jacob.

The boy dashed into the house to search for his mom.

"What's going on, Drew? Why are you looking so stressed?"

Drew had to blurt it out. "I'm going to be a father." He didn't need to ease into things with his cousin. Besides, he couldn't hold it inside any longer. Once he said it aloud, it became more real.

"That's great, Drew. I'm happy for you. I didn't know you were even seeing anyone, though." Derek said.

Derek knew about surprises. Jasmine had been his childhood sweetheart and circumstances had kept them apart until recently a year and a half ago. Once they'd found each other again — not under the best of circumstances — Derek discovered that he had a nine year old son. He'd been furious at first over the lost time and vowed not to lose any more. He'd married Jasmine in anger, but after that initial anger had faded, he'd realized how much he still loved Jacob's mother.

They'd overcome brutal misunderstandings, and now they were married and had a daughter as well.

Drew wouldn't be surprised if they had two more kids in the near future. They both loved being parents.

"I'm still in shock. You remember the girl I told you about five months ago at my resort? Well, I decided to pay her a visit and found her extremely pregnant. She wasn't going to tell me. To top it all off, she was planning on getting married to her best friend. I can't even describe what I feel right now. Anger — shock — joy. It's all there."

"I do understand." Derek said with a chuckle, causing Drew to send a glare his way. "Just be careful of what you do now, Drew, because you don't want to spook her. That's your baby she has, and you're lucky to have found her so soon. Just think, in a few months you'll be watching your son or daughter come into this world."

"It's a girl. I'm having a daughter."

"That's so great." Derek slapped Drew on the back.

When Jasmine stepped through the doors with Britney in her arms, Drew immediately held his own arms out to take the child. He couldn't seem to get enough of holding her. He couldn't even imagine how it would feel holding his own daughter.

"What's so great?" Jasmine asked him as she handed Britney over.

Drew immediately began blowing bubbles on her stomach, making her giggle in her tiny baby voice.

"I'm going to be a father," Drew replied. Jasmine was an amazing woman and he was glad she and Derek had managed to find each other again. Hell, he hadn't thought it was possible to find a woman as great as she was — OK, until he'd met Trinity.

"That's wonderful news, Drew." Jasmine threw her arms around his neck and kissed him on the cheek. "Why have I not met this woman?"

Jasmine wasn't happy he hadn't introduced them yet. But Drew's explanations calmed her sisterly wrath.

"I insist on meeting her right away," she told him.

Figuring that it would be good to have Jasmine on his side, Drew gave her the address of Trinity's floral shop. He knew it wouldn't take long for Jasmine to introduce herself. Family meant a lot to her, and Trinity was carrying a Titan child.

"You boys watch the kids while I make a celebratory dinner," Jasmine said as she turned toward the kitchen. "And for once, I won't make you help me."

The two men sat down, with Britney still in Drew's arms. She let out a slight yawn and closed her eyes. Continuing to rub along her tiny back, he smiled as she let out a sigh. He couldn't believe that in only a few short months he'd be doing the same thing with his own daughter. He'd never thought he'd want to be a father — he'd espoused a bachelor's total freedom for many a year — but the knowledge that he was about to have a child completely changed the way he felt. He could hardly wait for the joyous responsibility.

Derek gave his cousin time alone, almost, with his thoughts, and joined Jacob back in the pool, their laughter echoing off the walls. Drew sat and watched as Derek and Jacob continued their splashing war. He knew he'd been right to come over. As he finally started to relax, he could beging making plans for how he'd win Trinity over. He was a businessman — he could win any battle. Heck, a marriage was nothing more than a merger. He could negotiate terms that would suit both of their needs.

"Dinner will be ready in ten minutes, so get cleaned up," Jasmine called out from the other room. The boys didn't have to be told twice. Jacob and Derek scrambled from the pool and headed to the changing room. They were back out well within the time granted, and the three of them walked inside.

"Let me put her to bed so you can eat," Jasmine said as she held out her arms. Chortling at Drew's obvious reluctance to give the baby up, she said, "You can hold her again after dinner. Besides, she's asleep and just lying there, anyway."

"I love it when she's asleep and all cuddly. There's nothing like a beautiful lady lying across my chest," he said with a waggle of his brows.

Jasmine slapped his arm, then walked into the den to lay Britney down in her portable crib.

The rest of the crew enjoyed a nice meal together, and Drew got caught up on what he'd missed the last few weeks. He'd been growing tired of traveling for some time, but now that he was going to be a father, it was time to really think about settling down.

He needed to find a place, somewhere with a huge yard for a child to play in. For that matter, it would be best if he could find a house near his cousin. He wanted the kids to grow up together, the way he, Derek, and Ryan had. Familiarity and proximity bred a solid bond like no other.

After they finished eating, Drew sat in the den and had a drink while he waited for Derek and Jasmine to get the kids ready for bed. Derek joined him after a bit and the two men sat for a while, relaxing and talking business — at first.

Then Derek cut to the chase. "What are you going to do next?"

"I'm going to marry her, although convincing her of that may be a bit difficult since she won't even talk to me," Drew answered.

"Yeah, I've certainly been there."

"I should have told her the truth about who I was from the beginning, but it was nice to have a woman like me for myself, just thinking that I was just an everyday resort worker," Drew told his cousin.

Derek couldn't help but understand what Drew felt, considering where they'd come from and where they'd ended up. They'd been incredibly poor growing up, and many people had looked down their noses at them. Now that they were wealthy, too many people wanted to be with them for what they could get.

"Sometimes money is a real curse," Drew said.

"It will all work out. Take your time and be patient — unlike me. I lost a lot of years because of foolish pride. Time is one thing you can never get back, no matter how rich you become. Obviously the two of you have a connection that goes beyond the child that you'll both have; I've seen the way you've been acting since you met the woman. Don't go rushing off and acting like a crazy man," Derek said.

After the cousins said their goodnights, Drew made his way to the apartment above the garage and lay awake for hours. His mind wouldn't shut off and allow him to sleep. He was anxious to talk to Trinity again, make sure the day really had been real. Finally, sometime around morning's first light, he drifted off.

CHAPTER ELEVEN

TRINITY EMERGED FROM her apartment and walked down the stairs. Exhaustion seemed to be etched into her very bones. She'd tossed and turned the entire night, thinking about Drew and about what was going to happen next. She was still beyond angry with the man. He'd lied to her, lied because he was afraid she'd sue his precious resort.

Even if he'd been worried about the resort, he didn't need to play out the whole seduction thing. It was downright insulting. If he'd still been in her apartment in the morning, she might have thrown a mug at him. She hoped that he'd come to his senses and run away.

Nope. Trinity should have known she wasn't ever that lucky. When she looked up, her gaze collided with Drew's. He was leaning against an expensive vehicle — of course! — and he greeted her with an arrogant smile on his face.

As she studied him in his custom-made Armani suit, she couldn't believe she'd ever believed he was only a resort worker. She wasn't stupid, so there was only one explanation: she must have been really shaken up over her ex-boyfriend's betrayal.

Drew exuded raw masculine power, from the tips of his two-thousand-dollar loafers, to the cut of his expertly done hair. She knew she needed to put a wall between them, or she could easily fall under his spell once again.

So she pretended to ignore him and began walking down the street. Maybe if she pretended he wasn't there, he'd take a hint and disappear.

Yeah, right. She wasn't that lucky. He quickly caught up to her and didn't look too happy about being ignored. At least he'd lost the smug expression.

"You know we need to have a talk," Drew said.

She continued walking, choosing not to acknowledge his presence. Yes, her behavior might seem childish, but she didn't care. It was her prerogative, and he deserved the worst she could dish out.

"I'm not going away, and the longer you pretend like I'm not here, the longer you're going to have me trailing you," he said through clenched teeth.

Now this wasn't good. Trinity in no way wanted to have a confrontation with him so close to her shop. There were a lot of people about, people who didn't need to hear her personal business. But what could she do? She continued walking, and once she reached her shop, she unlocked the door and went inside.

He remained right on her heels.

As soon as they made it past the double doors, he seemed to have had enough. He grabbed her arm and spun her around. The look of fury on his face halted her protest. He was an intimidating sight.

"I'm trying to talk to you," he growled.

She tried to pull her arm away and realized it was useless. It was amazing how he could grip her so tightly without hurting her. And she really didn't like the way her body responded to the smallest touch from him — even when she was angry. She was far from over the man who'd hurt her so badly. Like every other man she'd known.

"I don't see what we have to talk about, Drew. You were worried about your resort, so you romanced me. I was feeling impulsive for the first and only time in my life, and I was a willing body, one who practically jumped into your bed — or, to be more precise, into your pool, at least the first and the critical time. Just because we didn't use a condom doesn't mean we become one big happy family. My child isn't for sale and neither am I," she snapped.

"I never once tried to buy you, and if you think I'd ever walk away from my child, you're sadly mistaken," he snapped back.

How would she know what he would or wouldn't do? She'd spent only one week with him. Granted, it had been the most memorable week of her life, but the math here was easy. One week was only seven days. But she still had a bad feeling that she wouldn't ever forget him, child or not. It had already been five months and she still had erotic dreams involving the wretched man.

"This is my child; make no mistake about that," she said through tight lips. And she was proud of saying that, proud of the person she was becoming. In her past life, she would have been reduced to a puddle of cheap grape jelly by the look on his face. She'd always been the first to back down —hell, she'd almost invited people to walk over her. Maybe it was the pregnancy that had brought out her fiercely protective instincts.

"We'll get married, Trinity." It was a demand.

She looked at him as if he'd lost his mind. Marry him? No way. He was everything she'd vowed to stay away from in a man. If she did marry, it would be to someone like Damien, someone kind and understanding. It was bad enough that Drew oozed self-satisfied machismo and masculine entitlement. But it was more serious than that. She refused to marry someone who had openly deceived her, and she wouldn't shackle herself to anyone, jerk or not, just because he'd gotten her pregnant.

"You need to understand this really quickly, *Mr. Titan*, I won't marry you, *ever*." She tugged at her arm again. Though he wasn't hurting her, his grip was firm and he didn't seem to be in any hurry to let her go.

"You didn't call me *Mr. Titan* when you were crying out my name as I sank deep inside you," he said. Her use of the formal name offended him far more than her words did.

Her eyes, already narrow, turned into brutally straight lines. She didn't need to be reminded of how she'd behaved on that wretched island. There must have been something in the water, because she'd done things there that she'd never even begin to think about doing in the real world.

"I didn't know that was who you were," she told him.

"You're seriously the most frustrating woman I've ever had to deal with," he shouted at her.

"Then stop dealing with me and go away," she yelled back.

They glared at one another, neither willing to back down. They were both breathing hard as the silence dragged on.

To hell with this, Drew thought. He pulled her up against him and crushed his lips to hers.

She was too shocked to react at first, and stood in his arms like a rag doll as his tongue rubbed across her lips, seeking entrance.

When she finally came out of her shock, she pushed against him for about three seconds, but heat started pooling in her stomach and thighs. She hadn't been kissed like that for five months, and her hormones were all over the place. And as his lips continued to stroke hers, anger changed to all-consuming passion. She couldn't even think about what his hands were doing as they rubbed up and down her body.

Drew's fit of temper seemed to have evaporated as he continued caressing her, and he heard her gasp as a current of electricity shot down to her core, making her knees go weak. The gasp was all he needed to slip his tongue inside her mouth. He tangled his tongue greedily with hers, and she could have done Dante's *Inferno* proud.

She was no longer trying to push him away. Heck, she was clutching at him, molding his body to hers as best she could. As he deepened the kiss, she forgot about the fight, about her anger, even about who she was. His hands moved down to grip her backside and pull her against his very obvious arousal. *Outstanding* was a good word for it. Her stomach was sticking out, but not so far yet that she couldn't feel his impressive erection sticking out into her. Oh, she wanted him.

He backed her up against the counter and lifted her up so he could slide between her legs. Their lips remained glued together; he refused to break contact. He needed it, desperately.

She'd never been so devoured in her life, and she had no desire for it to end. There really was a very thin line between anger and passion, and she'd crossed over it without a thought.

He spread her legs farther apart, pressing himself closer to her aching heat as he continued with the heart-stopping kiss. Her hands circled his neck, while her fingers dove into his thick hair, and she tugged on the strands. Closer, please, closer. He growled in his throat as he gladly obliged her unspoken request.

In the back of Trinity's mind, there was a voice shouting for her to stop, but she didn't want to listen. She wanted to keep feeling the exquisite pleasure he was bringing to her body. It — no, she — needed him so much.

He slipped his hand underneath her blouse and ran his fingers over the bump of her stomach and up to her heavy breasts. She groaned desperately as he rubbed a finger over her nipples, which were poking through the thin covering of her bra. He pinched the pebbled buds, and she almost came apart right there on the shop's counter. She'd responded to him readily and easily before, but it was nothing in comparison to what was happening now.

He moved his hands down to her skirt and started rucking it up, pushing it out of his way. It was obvious they'd both forgotten they were in a public place, a place where anyone could walk in at any time. But she couldn't help it. She needed to relieve the intense pressure building up in her body. She needed this. She deserved this. What could one more time hurt? After all, she couldn't get pregnant again right now. That ship had sailed.

The jarring sound of the phone brought Trinity back to reality. It kept ringing, and she pulled back, realizing where she was and what she was doing. Looking into Drew's desire-filled eyes, she gasped. He was still holding her close and bending his head to join her lips again with his.

The phone had done nothing to call him back to the real world. His desire was undampened, and he was ready to continue where they'd left off. Without realizing what she was doing, she raised her hand and slapped him hard across the cheek. The sound echoed through the small shop and Trinity sat there, stunned at what she'd just done. She stared at him open-mouthed, speechless in her shock.

The slap seemed to clear his head. He took a step back and stared at her. She couldn't help but see his anger simmering away.

"Did you get it all out?" His voice had a deadly calm to it, which was far more frightening to her than if he'd been yelling.

She had her hand still clasped over her mouth. She really hadn't meant to slap him. She couldn't blame him for the kissing, as she had done nothing to stop it — well, until the phone rang. She was still furious with him, but she'd been just as excited as he had.

"I…I didn't mean to do that," she finally managed to say.

He rubbed his cheek and raised his eyebrows.

"It sure as hell feels like you meant to do it, and you put your full weight into it," he said with a smirk. He was quickly regaining his composure and once again acting like the one in control.

She narrowed her eyes, knowing full well that his remark about her increasing weight had been pointed. She put her hand across her stomach, reminding them both she carried a child in there.

"I'll be back," Drew told her. "This discussion is in no way over."

What he said seemed far more like a threat than anything else. She stayed silent as he stomped out the door.

CHAPTER TWELVE

STORMING DOWN THE street did nothing to work off Drew's frustration. He'd never in his life been at such a fever pitch. But he had to get a grip. Though he still wanted her with a need that was frightening in its intensity, he needed to set that aside.

She was carrying his child, and that meant marriage. It simply had to be. Some decades ago, he could have simply dragged her down the aisle and made her his bride, and he'd have been far happier that way. These stupid games were wearing him out.

He wasn't a man used to being told no, and he found he didn't like it much. He hadn't expected her to fall into his arms at first glance, but he certainly hadn't expected her continuing hostility. He'd messed up with one small lie, and she'd just have to get over it.

No problem, really. She had to be like other women; she had her price. He'd support her comfortably, with all those little things women liked — shoes, jewelry, whatever — and in turn he'd get to be there to raise his child.

The thought of her with another man whom his child would call dad? Not effing likely. He was the baby's father, and no other man would play that role.

He stopped at a local pub and ordered a double bourbon. He never drank so early in the morning, but unless he wanted to walk the streets with an obvious arousal, he needed something to soothe his desire and his temper. Damn, he couldn't think about what she did to him. His mind shut down the second he touched her, every single time. Marriage wasn't looking too bad, not at all.

Normally, he forgot a woman as soon as he walked out her door. He enjoyed women. He loved their soft curves, their scent, even their laughter. He loved everything about them, but he never got hung up on just one silly female. Why was he so fixated on her? It didn't seem possible, but he hadn't so much as touched another woman since his time with Trinity. They all paled in comparison to her. Hell, he'd gladly throw away millions of dollars for one more night in her arms. Despite his massive wealth, he knew the value of money.

He signaled the bartender and ordered another drink. He had a feeling it was going to be a very long day, and he was preparing for round two with Trinity. He had to smile at her spunk, though, because he had a feeling that being married to her was never going to get boring. Cheered up at last, he finally managed to leave the bar and do things that were marginally productive.

Several hours later, he decided it was time. He arrived at her shop feeling much calmer, and ready for the challenge of this new round.

But signs weren't in his favor. When he walked in the door, and she glanced up to see who it was, he watched as she went back to what she was doing as if he weren't there. Sheesh.

This was getting tiresome in the extreme, but he knew what to do. He strode over to her work station and stood by her side with his body rubbing against hers. He knew she couldn't ignore him if he was touching her. He wouldn't mind finishing what they had started earlier, anyway.

She finally snapped at him. "You're invading my space!"

He smiled as he heard the tension in her voice. His presence clearly affected her more than she wanted to admit.

"But, darling, we should most definitely get used to touching, as we're going to be married," he came back with.

"I'm not going to marry you." Trinity spoke slowly, as if she were talking to a child.

"Then the neighbors are going to talk about your shabby morals when they know you're my mistress," he told her. "Our child will be looked down upon because her mother is shacking up."

* * *

Dammit. She was destroying innocent and expensive flowers. There was no point in working on this stupid arrangement. Trinity knew that Drew was only trying to rile her up, and she refused to let him ruin any more of her work. She began putting things away and looked yet again at the clock. Virtually no change. She still had a few hours to go before she could close the shop. Given a choice, she'd have stormed out, away from his toxic presence, but it wouldn't do her much good, anyway, as he'd most likely follow her.

"I'm not going to be living with you, so that won't be a problem," she finally calmed down enough to say. It still came out between clenched teeth, but at least she wasn't shouting.

"I'm going to be a full-time father, so we're going to be

together — one way or the other."

She threw up her hands and stomped off to the bathroom. And she stayed in there for a while, trying to figure out what she was going to do about the miserable man.

She finally emerged to find Drew at the counter with a woman who was apparently buying one of the larger bouquets for sale from her display case. The woman was flirting openly with Drew, and Trinity was surprised to feel a coil of jealousy in her gut.

What was going on here? She didn't want to be with him, and she didn't care who he flirted with. But when the woman let out a giggle and fluttered her eyelashes like some second-rate southern belle, Trinity had to fight the urge to smack her.

"It was so great to meet you, and I hope you have a wonderful time at your mother's house," he told the…female with a disgustingly coming smile. The woman actually blushed, and when she turned around and left, Trinity could hardly believe it.

She stood there with her mouth hanging open as Drew turned to face her.

"I used to work at a little hardware store when I was a teenager," he said. "Luckily, your register was similar to that one, so I took care of the sale."

He handed over the receipt and saw Trinity's eyes open at the amount he'd charged. "I wasn't sure how much you were selling the bouquet for," he said nervously, "so I took a guess from some I've purchased before. I hope it was correct."

"No, you actually sold it for twice the amount I would have normally charged." She was shocked the woman had paid so much. Hey, maybe she should hire a majorly attractive guy to work in her shop. If this was any indication, her sales would skyrocket.

"Seriously? You're charging too little for your arrangements, then."

"I don't need business advice, Drew," she snapped. He had a point, but she was worried she'd lose customers by inflating her fees. She'd rather have a lot of customers who were paying less than take the risk that he was suggesting. Gambling wasn't in her blood, even if it meant working fewer hours

While she was pondering the bottom line, he changed the subject completely.

"I hope you've come to your senses by now. I can arrange a wedding within a couple of days, a week at most."

His conversation tone and overconfidence stunned her. How could he criticize her one second and talk about marrying her in the next? He really needed someone to come along and knock him off of his pedestal. She was more than willing to be the one to do it.

"OK, Drew, I'm going to tell you this for the last time, and I hope you'll finally hear it. I'm not going to marry you. What happened on the island was a mistake, which means it shouldn't have taken place. After the baby is born, we'll talk about visitation, but right now she's in my stomach and mine alone, so you can go ahead and leave for the next four months."

She walked purposefully to the front door, pulled it open, and looked at him expectantly. He returned her look with narrowed eyes, and she could see he was struggling to decide what to do.

He finally walked to the door and pressed his body up close to hers, causing her heart rate to quicken and her breathing to grow shallow. She glared at him, angry at how easily he made her melt. He smiled for a couple of seconds, then bent down and kissed her. It happened so fast that she had no time to react. It was a short kiss, but it seemed to tell her that he really was the one with all the power. Her worst fear was that he might be right.

"I'll be back," he told her with promise.

She stood there, frozen. As she watched him walk down the street, she felt a mixture of relief and sadness. She was determined to protect herself, but he was so confident, and he had so much sex appeal that it was hard for her to remember who she even was when he was around.

She closed the door and went back to work. She had a wedding coming up — not hers! — and it was a lot of work getting all the arrangements ready. At least it wasn't prom season, she thought with relief. The money was always good, but her hands were done for by the end.

Drew climbed into his car. His forceful approach obviously wasn't working, so he was going to have to try something new. His father had always liked to say that you caught more flies with honey than with vinegar, so maybe he needed to change his methods of trying to catch this little honey. Of course, he really didn't understand that saying, since he didn't know why anyone would want to catch flies. He drove to his hotel and started forging a new game plan.

CHAPTER THIRTEEN

TRINITY TOOK HER time getting ready for the new day. She knew only too well that when she set foot outside of her tiny apartment, Drew would be there, and she didn't know how long she'd be able to resist him. She was OK when he was being demanding and arrogant, but when he turned on the sex appeal, she was a goner. She was hoping he'd take the hint and disappear for a while so she didn't have to fight him, and herself, too.

The baby kicked her hard in the ribs, as if the little girl didn't like the her mother's thoughts. Trinity rubbed her stomach and whispered soothingly to her daughter.

Nowadays, she was always starving in the morning, but she didn't have the energy to fix anything, so she grabbed a muffin and poured herself a large glass of milk to nibble on as she finished getting ready for the day.

Lately, the hours at her shop were dragging on painfully. When she had no customers around, she was starting to feel lonely. Having company, just having another person around would be a major plus. She really needed to hire someone, but she didn't want to pay wages until she absolutely had to. She was thinking it might be a better idea to work for someone else for a while, so she could at least be around other people, co-workers instead of employees, and not have to worry about payroll. Even though it had been her dream to own her own place, it wasn't as fulfilling as she'd thought it would be.

Finally, Trinity stepped outside and glanced around the corner. Drew wasn't there. As she walked the few blocks to her shop, she noticed she was looking in every direction, and found herself a bit disappointed not to see him. Just that thought made her scowl. She didn't want him around, and she needed to always remember that. If she felt a little disappointment now, it had to be her hormones.

She turned her key in the lock and flipped the open sign around. She normally felt instant pride when walking through the front doors. She'd worked hard to make her dream come true, and had felt satisfaction in owning the small but beautiful shop. Her touch was present in every square inch of the room. That sensation of something missing was taking a little of that feeling away, though.

She put her purse away and stepped around to the floral station so she could begin making bouquets for walk-in customers. She had a few orders for delivery, but other than that, it was a slow day.

The bell over her door rang, and she looked up to see Drew striding inside, looking way too good for so early in the morning. She should have known he wouldn't wait long before stalking her again. She was surprised, though, by the instant quickening of her heart.

"Good morning. How are you today?" he asked, as if they were strangers.

She looked at him suspiciously, wondering what he was up

to.

"I'm fine. And you?"

"I'm feeling pretty great. I'm in need of several bouquets." He stuck out his hand. "My name is Andrew Titan, but my friends call me Drew. I own several vacation resorts, and I'm in need of a new florist," he said with a straight face.

"What are you up to, Drew?"

"I decided we need to start over from scratch, so here I am, being completely honest," he told her with a twinkle in his eyes.

She found it hard to resist him when he was acting so charming. She decided to play along for at least a few minutes.

"It's nice to meet you, Drew. I'd love to help you with your 'floral needs,'" she said and took his still-outstretched hand. She wasn't prepared for the fire that shot down her arm. She tried pulling away, but he held on tight. The man should have a warning label attached to him. He was a serious threat to the female libido.

"The pleasure is all mine," he said in the sexiest voice she'd ever heard.

"What kind of arrangements do you need?" She finally managed to pull her hand free. Not easy at all. She had to resist the urge to rub it against her leg.

"I'll leave that up to you. I have three orders I need to send to prospective investors, and I want to send a huge bouquet to my cousin's wife. She gave birth a while ago and I realized I never sent flowers. That kid is the cutest thing ever, and she deserves the biggest arrangement you can possibly make."

Trinity was surprised by his request. He'd gone all soft eyed while talking about the baby. She'd never taken him for the kind of guy who loved babies. Maybe she really didn't know him all that well.

She walked over to her cooler and started selecting flowers.

Drew followed her around and lifted the buckets; he insisted on transporting them to her workstation. She tried to shoo him away, but he was determined.

"I've been lifting these buckets just fine on my own," she said when he got in her way for the tenth time.

"You need to take care of yourself." He looked pointedly at her stomach.

OK, OK. She figured it was easier to let him help than continue to argue.

"How long have you had this place?"

"I opened a couple years ago. It was always my dream. I'd like to expand someday and have a larger shop, with gift items and live plants, as well."

"Is the store successful?"

"I'm doing a lot better than I thought I would. With the baby coming, though, I'm going to have to hire help, and that will cut into the profits."

"I know it's difficult for small businesses to succeed," he said.

"I'm doing better than some." Why not accentuate the positive? That's what she'd been trying to do for years.

"Your work is beautiful. You have a real gift," he told her, amused that she was keeping her head down and working. Was she attempting to avoid him?

"Thank you, I really enjoy doing it." She was human and always liked to receive a little praise for her arrangements. Each one was like a new art project. It was highly depressing when the flowers wilted away, though.

The two of them continued to chat easily and companionably as she finished with his order. He sat there on a stool, continuing to visit with her when a few customers came and went. She was enjoying it more than she should. She knew she should have asked him to leave, but it was nice having company. The time was passing quickly and they'd managed not to fight for a few hours straight.

And she had to face the fact that they should at least be friends. If she could manage to control her temper, plus the hunger she felt every time she was around him, it might be a possibility.

"I need to close down for a while and make deliveries," she finally said. She normally did her deliveries at the end of her shift, but she had a whopper of an order to get to a funeral.

"Why don't I do the deliveries for you, Trinity, so you can go ahead and stay open?"

She had been busy all morning, and the businesswoman in her was well aware that closing the shop wasn't ideal, but she didn't want to feel as if she owed Drew anything.

Trinity's reluctance was almost palpable, and Drew almost laughed. But his amusement didn't show in what he said. "I don't mind, really. I have some stops to make, anyway."

"If you really don't mind…" How could she help but cave?

He took down the addresses, loaded up her orders, and took off. She was a bit sad to see him leave. She had to shake it off, refusing to get attached to him being around. Luckily for her, the phone rang, distracting her, then customers continued coming through the doors. She didn't have any more time to get lost in her thoughts, or stress about spending time with Drew.

By the time he walked in the door — oh, my, he was holding a sack that looked unassuming, but the aromas coming out of it made her stomach growl possessively — she realized she was starving. He set the sack on the counter, and she practically ripped it apart in her desperation to see what was inside. She pulled out a takeout container holding her favorite pasta dish and could feel the saliva building up in her mouth.

She dove in with real enthusiasm. She didn't say anything

until she was about halfway finished with the meal. And then she finally looked up. Oh, no! He was staring at her with a huge smile on his face. How humiliating.

"Sorry. Sometimes I get so busy, I forget to eat. Then, when I see food, I go a little crazy," she said as her embarrassment tinged her cheeks with pink.

His eyes darkened in memory. "You were like that on the island."

She reacted in turn to thoughts of the resort. It had been a tropical paradise, and she hadn't thought of anything but pleasure. The pleasure of the sun, the water, the food, and most especially, the pleasure of her body when he was touching her.

"That was a million years ago, Drew," she said. "I'm back in the real world now, and have real-world responsibilities. I do appreciate your help today, and the pasta, too, but we're over and you need to accept that." She was trying to convince herself of that fact as much as she was trying to convince him.

Drew's expression didn't change a bit. He continued to stare at her with longing in his eyes, which was doing strange things to her stomach. She tried to focus on the food, but her appetite was gone. She was hungry for something much more satisfying. She picked at the pasta dish a little more, but she finally had to give up, and she shoved it aside.

Drew gently grabbed her hand and waited until he had her full attention.

"I won't back down on this. You simply have to become my wife. I've never felt about a woman the way I feel about you. Add to that the fact that you're carrying my child and it means we'll stay together. I understand you're scared. I know you're angry I misled you, but you'll realize you can't live without me. I'm irresistible."

She was left breathless and without any words. It was almost impossible to argue with the man, but as she thought about what he said, her temper flared. How dare he demand such things of her? She wasn't his mistress, a weak, helpless bimbo put on earth only to please him.

"Drew, sometimes in life you simply have to accept it when you can't have your own way," she said with some venom. "I'm not a possession you get to choose to keep or cast off. You've irritated me now, and I'd like for you to leave."

Drew laughed. She couldn't believe that the man had actually laughed at her.

"You're so good for me, Trinity. I need people in my life who aren't afraid to tell me how it is — but nonetheless, we *will* be together. I have more errands to run, but I'll be back before you close." Almost as an afterthought, he kissed her gently, and he walked out the door.

Trinity stood stock still for several minutes, with her hand pressed against her still-tingling lips. Drew had a way of keeping her off kilter. But she finally shook it off and got back to work. When he did return, she'd have to be firm and avoid physical contact, even if she had to put on a suit of armor.

CHAPTER FOURTEEN

A BOUT AN HOUR before closing, Trinity heard the bell on the door ring, letting her know someone was coming in. She looked up nervously, then let out a sigh of relief, followed by a pang of disappointment, when it was a woman, not Drew.

"Welcome to the store. How may I help you?" Trinity asked.

"For starters, you can make the day a little longer, so I can have more sleep?" the woman said with a laugh.

"I would gladly do that if I could." As Trinity spoke, she rubbed her protruding stomach. The women shared a look of understanding.

"My name's Jasmine, and this little one is Britney," the woman said, and she held out her free hand.

"It's nice to meet you, Jasmine. I'm Trinity. Are you looking for something special?" She loved customers like Jasmine, who were happy and friendly.

"Actually, I just wanted to meet you. I'm married to Derek Titan, Drew's cousin," Jasmine said.

"Oh…well…um…" Trinity could do no more than stutter.

"I know," Jasmine said. "I shouldn't have just barged in here on you, but when Drew told us he was going to be a father, I had to meet the woman who finally captured him." Her friendly smile took away the shock of her words.

Trinity started to protest. "We aren't together, though…"

Jasmine broke in. "You're carrying a Titan child, so you're pretty much together, believe me. You can try and fight it, but these guys really care about family. My husband and I had a very rocky start, but I'm over the top in love with him now. I'm incredibly grateful he fought for me, because now we have Britney and Jacob, and I'm disgustingly happy all the time."

The baby was squirming in her arms, and Trinity wanted to hold the cute little thing, but she didn't even know this woman. She couldn't just ask her to hand over her child. But Jasmine saw the look of yearning on Trinity's face and held Britney out to her. Trinity gently pulled the child into her arms and laughed when Britney smiled up at her.

"She's so precious," Trinity whispered.

Jasmine's look of baby love was also precious. "She's pretty amazing, and incredibly spoiled."

"Why don't you sit with me over here so we can visit?" Trinity moved to the love seat she'd brought in when she found out about her pregnancy.

"That sounds perfect," Jasmine told her. "I want to hear all about how you and Drew met. Don't leave out any of the juicy details."

Trinity could feel the heat suffuse her cheeks as she thought about those details. She didn't know why it was, but she liked Jasmine. Maybe she was lonelier than she thought, especially with Damien out of town on business.

Trinity found herself opening up about her time on the island, and then about the last few days. Jasmine listened attentively the whole time, nodding her head in understanding.

"Seriously, I know he's behaved like a complete moron," Jasmine said, "but he's a terrific guy, and if you give him a chance, you'll see that."

"I'm sure he's great, but I've sworn off all men. My last relationship was a disaster, and the one before that. I wouldn't even call what happened with Drew and me a relationship. It was more like spontaneous combustion. I won't try and keep the baby from him, but I can't get into a relationship with him," Trinity said. She hoped Jasmine would understand.

"I'm sure it will all work out," Jasmine said, and the woman looked completely confident.

The bell rang again, and in walked the man in question. It didn't take him long to spot the two women.

"There's my beautiful girl," Drew said as he approached.

Just as Trinity was starting to blush, he plucked the baby out of her arms. Britney immediately started to giggle and Trinity felt her blush deepen because she'd stupidly thought that the comment had been for her. She hoped he hadn't noticed.

"Uncle missed you, precious." He cuddled Britney and continued to talk to her. She looked up at him as if she could understand every word.

Trinity was impressed with how well he handled the baby. If he turned out to be half as affectionate with his own daughter, she'd always know her father loved her.

Jasmine glared at him. "You have a lot to make up for, Drew."

"What?" he asked as he looked from one woman to the other, and he shook his head at the contemptuous looks he was getting from both of them. He looked back down at Britney. "At least you don't look at Uncle that way," he said.

Trinity almost cracked a smile — he was pretty adorable with a baby in his arms.

"I can't believe what a moron you were at the resort," Jasmine remarked. "Seriously, Drew. you bonked her in the head and then had the gall to lie to her. No wonder she's giving you a hard time." Turning, Jasmine altered her tone. "It was so great to meet you, Trinity. Please come have lunch with me on your next day off. I want to get to know you more, and I really want the kids to grow up together."

"I think that sounds wonderful. I'll be off on Sunday and Monday, if either of those days works for you," Trinity replied.

Jasmine grabbed a little card and started to scribble. "Sunday will be perfect. Come any time after ten. Here's my address and phone number. I can't wait to see you." She gathered her baby up and headed out.

Trinity looked over at the clock and was relieved it was closing time. She counted out her till and started shutting things down.

"Can I take you to dinner, please?" Drew asked.

She knew she should probably say no. She found she wanted to spend time with him, though, which was frightening. She was really trying to get the word *no* to come out of her mouth. Sure she was.

"That sounds fine" was what she said.

They walked out of the shop and he immediately grabbed her hand. She fought for a moment to pull free, but he was holding firm, so she gave up. It was much easier to let go of the smaller battles so she had the energy for the bigger arguments.

"How was your day, Trinity?"

"Busy. I had an unusual amount of customers. It's good, though, because I really need to save as much as possible so I can afford help after the baby's born."

"You won't be doing it alone, sweetheart. I'm not going to stand by and watch you work yourself to death when I have endless funds available."

She could hear the frustration in his tone, but she didn't want to take from him. She wanted to prove she was able to do it all on her own.

As they walked down the street, she was trying to remember her reasons for insisting on that independence. The feel of his hand in hers was nice. She wanted to lean into him and let him take some of the weight off her shoulders. That would make her weak, though, wouldn't it?

The silence had dragged on too long, and she had to say something. "Why do you have to argue with me so much, Drew?"

"I wouldn't have to if you'd just do things my way," he quickly replied.

Trinity smiled, then laughed. He really was hard to stay irritated with, especially when he put the full force of his charm out there.

"Where are we going?"

"There's a terrific Italian restaurant down the block. It's a nice night, so I thought we'd just walk."

"I've eaten there before. It's good." She was glad it wasn't far; after all, her feet were done in. And they arrived at the little eatery early enough to beat the crowds, so they got seated right away.

"So, Drew, what are all these errands you run all day?"

"A little of this and that," he remarked as he looked at his menu.

"Are you secretly a drug dealer?" That got his attention. He looked up with startled eyes, until he realized she was kidding.

Then he gave her one of his full-blown smiles, and she was glad she was sitting down, because her knees became instantly weak.

"Me? A dealer? Only on the weekends," he answered. Their waiter came and they paused to place their order. Her stomach growled loudly as the man turned to leave.

"Ever since I became pregnant, I can't stop eating. I'm going to gain a hundred pounds at this rate," she said, thoroughly embarrassed.

"You look like you could eat a lot more."

"OK, back to the errands. What do you do?"

"I'm sick of traveling. I've been doing it for ten years, and it's lost the appeal it once had. I could retire if I wanted, but I love what I do, so I've been looking at some places around town where I could open up an architecture firm. I haven't made any decisions yet."

"Oh." Trinity could only look at him. This was getting worse and worse. If he was in town all the time, that meant he'd be around her a lot more. She'd been having too much trouble resisting him already, and if he was in her face constantly, she'd be doomed.

Their appetizers arrived, saving her from having to respond. The way he was looking at her told her that he wanted her input, but what could she say? She should talk about how much he'd miss the constant travel. She should try to convince him how much better the open road was. She shouldn't want him to be here — but she did.

After they finished their dinner, Trinity decided she needed a hot shower and then bed. Alone, of course. She could think about her situation with Drew when she had a full night's rest behind her, not when she could barely stand.

He took her arm in his as he walked the short distance back to her apartment. Neither of them said a word as they neared the building, but she was starting to feel butterflies in her stomach. Was he going to kiss her goodnight, as if it had been a real date? Did she want him to? *Yes!* her body screamed.

"Thank you for dinner, Drew. It was great. I'm really tired, though, so I'm just going to head inside," she said at the bottom of the stairs. She didn't want him to come near her apartment. She was too afraid she'd invite him in.

"I'll walk you to the door," he said in a voice that let her know arguing would do no good.

Her shoulders slumped a little, but she moved forward, with him at her side.

"We're perfect together, Trinity. You know that, right? I can barely focus on anything when you're around, because all I'm thinking about is how to get you undressed. It's more than just sex, though. Surely you know that. You make me laugh. You intrigue me, and you have a great sense of humor. Our marriage won't get dull or predictable. We're good together, dammit." As he spoke, Drew turned her into his arms, his lips brushing hers with each word he spoke.

He didn't complete the kiss, just let his lips linger over hers. What was more seductive, his words or the physical torment, she wondered. Either way, shivers were racing down her spine. She wanted his mouth fully on hers.

"Think about how good it will be," he said, finally slipping his tongue across her lips.

She moaned as he gently nipped her. He moved his hand along her back until it reached her derrière. He applied pressure, pulling her against him as he trailed his mouth downward and gently sucked the sensitive skin of her neck.

To hell with caution. She needed him to come inside. And just as she was about to beg him to come in and finish what he'd started — he released her and took a step back. From the satisfied expression on his face, he knew exactly what state her body was in.

Thankfully, anger returned, and a need for payback.

"Night," she whispered as she unlocked the door. Right before she went inside, she brushed her hand down his stomach, her fingers sliding across his strained zipper. His gasp was the final sound she heard before her door clicked shut. Though she was about to burst at the seams, at least she was home. He had to walk down the block, then drive several miles, and all while wearing extremely tight pants.

Trinity smiled as she pushed away from the door and headed to her bathroom. If she wanted to get any sleep that night, she had to thrust him from her thoughts. Much easier said than done.

CHAPTER FIFTEEN

S UNDAY CAME QUICKLY, and Trinity found she was excited to see Jasmine again. She'd always had a hard time making friends, because she was so busy all the time, plus she was painfully shy. She was also the practical one. When other kids had been out partying, she'd been the one studying.

It had all been worth it, though, because she now owned her own shop, and was on her way to her goals getting accomplished. She was about ready to leave when a knock sounded on her door. She knew who it was before she opened it.

"Good morning," Drew said, and he walked right in.

She could smell the warm scent of muffins wafting through the bag he was holding. She'd have to talk to him about his compulsive need to feed her.

"I can take care of myself, you know." But she grabbed the bag and started munching on a delicious little quick bread. She didn't know where he bought them, but they were heavenly. She soon found herself halfway through a second one.

"I know you're more than capable of taking care of yourself, but I enjoy feeding you, and taking care of you. I've never been a father before and I want to make sure my daughter is getting all she needs," he explained.

Trinity rolled her eyes. "Yeah, right, a belly full of sugar and starch will really get the kid going. All I need — a hyperactive place-kicker."

She put on her jacket, which was getting too tight. Then she locked up and allowed him to walk her down the stairs.

"I'm visiting Derek today, so we can ride together," Drew told her as he steered her toward his car.

She didn't like his assuming she'd automatically come with him, but at least she wouldn't have to struggle to fit behind the wheel in her car. It was becoming harder with each passing day.

They rode to the place in a comfortable silence. Trinity was still trying to fully wake up, and Drew seemed to have something on his mind. She didn't mind. She hated trying to make polite conversation with anyone.

They made their way through the gate and started up the long driveway. As the home came into view, Trinity's jaw dropped.

"This is where they live?" She asked. It looked more like a resort than someone's home. Her eyes were drawn to the huge front doors and the seemingly endless walls. She didn't know how they managed to find their way anywhere inside the home. Floor maps at strategic intervals, each with a big YOU ARE HERE? Hospital signs, maybe?

"I know it's large. I gave Derek a heck of a time when I first saw it, but Jasmine's made it really homey," he told her.

She didn't see how it was possible to make the mansion look homey. It was simply too massive.

When he pulled up by the front doors and they climbed from the vehicle, a young boy came rushing out. "Uncle Drew, you're here!" he cried out, then he launched himself into Drew's arms.

"Hey, buddy. I think I'm going to whup you today in water basketball," Drew said as he ruffled the boy's hair.

"No way! I've been practicing. You're going down!"

Trinity had to smile at their banter.

"Jacob, this nice lady is Trinity," Drew said. "Trinity, this young lad is my nephew, Jacob."

"It's nice to meet you," the boy said politely.

"It's nice to meet you, as well," Trinity replied. He was adorable and well-mannered, especially for his age. He looked like he might be at that preteen stage.

"Mom is excited that you're coming. Follow me. She's in the kitchen," Jacob said, and he ran ahead of them, through the front doors. Trinity couldn't stop looking around her. She walked slowly at Drew's side as they made their way to the back of the house. She could hear laughter — was it Jasmine talking to the baby?

She could understand what Drew meant when he said the place was homey. Though it was as big as a small hotel, colorful throw pillows brightened up the furniture, and toys were scattered about. Instead of priceless pieces of art, the walls held family portraits and finger paintings. It was obviously a lived-in home, not a museum or a mausoleum.

"You guys made it. I'm so glad," Jasmine said as they stepped into the kitchen. She gave Drew a quick hug, then surprised Trinity by throwing her arms around her as well. She pulled back with a giggle. "I remember those days of my belly preceding me into a room."

She laughed again, and Trinity couldn't help but laugh with her.

"I know. I think I grow a foot every night."

"You boys go play so we can diss on you for a while," Jasmine commanded.

The men obeyed and left them alone. With the aroma of Jasmine's cooking in the air, Trinity's stomach let out a loud growl. Trinity couldn't believe she was still hungry after eating those rich muffins, but she couldn't seem to get enough.

"I remember that, too," Jasmine said. "You're in the stage of pregnancy where morning sickness is gone and you want to consume everything in sight. Sit down and let me give you a snack while everything finishes up."

"I can wait. I don't want to be a hassle."

"Oh, stop being so submissive. You have to learn to stand up for yourself, or seriously, these Titan guys will walk all over you." Jasmine went about fixing up a snack.

"You're right. I'd love to have something." Trinity didn't seem to have much choice anyway. If the Titan men were stubborn, Jasmine looked as if she fit right in.

"That's a start. Now, get off those feet and relax. Your ankles are pretty swollen. Have you had high blood pressure during the pregnancy?" Jasmine asked.

"Yes. It's a constant battle. I've cut out salt as much as possible. I've even managed to cut back to decaf tea and coffee, but I can't seem to get the swelling to stop. I don't know the history on my mother. She died when I was very young, so I can't ask her if she had the same symptoms."

"I'm sorry." Jasmine paused to take her hand.

"I don't remember her, so it's not a big deal. It would just be nice to know the medical stuff," Trinity said, though it did hurt at times to not have a mom to confide in.

"I'm not going to push you. I have my own parent issues, but if you need someone to talk to..." Jasmine trailed off.

Trinity just wanted to change the subject. "What is this? It's practically melting on my tongue," she said as she took the first bite of what Jasmine had put before her.

"Oh, that's just an easy recipe I made up. Cheese makes everything taste better," Jasmine said, obviously a little embarrassed.

"Trust me, I add cheese to everything and it never tastes this good. Are you a professional cook?"

"No, I just really love to create dishes. I've been doing it since I was young." Jasmine spoke with excitement, her embarrassment forgotten.

"You should seriously open up a café," Trinity told her.

"I've been told the same thing from these handsome men, but I don't want to lose my love of cooking," Jasmine said. "If I had to do it for the long hours it takes in order to succeed, I'd no longer enjoy it."

"You know, I've always wanted to open a floral and gift shop with a little café in it. I also thought it would be great to have a section of books people could buy — they could come in and eat, read, and order flowers. It's one-stop shopping. If you do ever consider a café, then I hope you'll talk to me," Trinity said shyly.

She hadn't admitted that to anyone besides Damien. He'd tried to fund the whole project for her, but she'd flat out refused. She still contemplated doing it someday, but she wasn't having her best friend foot the bill for her dream.

"Now that's something I'd consider, Trinity. It would be fun to get out of the house a few hours a day. I could have it open for breakfast and lunch only. Now you have the wheels turning in my head. Let me finish cooking our meal; then we can do some research."

"I meant in the future." Trinity tried to take a step back. It wasn't something she could even think about doing while pregnant.

"There's no time like the present," Jasmine said.

Trinity offered up a few more protests, but Jasmine was more determined than Drew. It seemed the Titan stubbornness was contagious. When it became abundantly clear that Jasmine wasn't backing off the idea, Trinity decided it couldn't hurt to just look at stuff…

The women continued talking while Jasmine cooked lunch. As if the men had built-in radar, they showed up just when everything was ready. They sat around the table, enjoying both the food and conversation.

Trinity found herself having a wonderful time, and she knew she'd be forever grateful to have met Jasmine.

"You boys are on cleanup duty. Trinity and I are going to the library to do research," Jasmine said mysteriously, and the two women took off.

"I know I shouldn't say this, Jasmine, but this house is huge. Do you keep it clean yourself?" Trinity's curiosity had simply gotten the better of her. Jasmine was cooking and the boys were cleaning. No help? How could she manage in this freaking palace?

"No. I'm sad to say, I'm not superwoman. I'd be much too worn out to be even a halfway-decent mom if I had to cook and clean this huge place all day. We have a small staff, but I insist on Sunday's being their day off. I want one day a week where it's just my family here. We have a great cook, too. I used to make her nervous because I'm always in the kitchen. We're very close now, though."

They made it to the library, and Trinity gasped. It was a stunning room, with books from floor to ceiling. She walked along the shelves, noticing titles both old and young, and seemingly in every genre.

"It's pretty great, huh? I still have a long way to go before these shelves are filled, but I get a few more each week. This library is what sold me on the place," Jasmine said.

They really did have a tremendous amount in common, Trinity thought. "This is amazing. I don't think I'd ever leave this library if I lived here."

"I feel the same way, at least when I'm not drawn to the kitchen. Take your time looking around. I'm going to jump on the computer and do research." Jasmine sat down on the comfortable-looking sofa and opened a laptop.

After a while, she pulled Trinity over to show her a building for sale. It looked absolutely perfect for what they wanted to do, but the price tag was extravagant.

"I don't think I can afford that," Trinity had to say. Damn.

"Let's not worry about the cost right now. I know how that sounds, but let's just look at it tomorrow and see what we think." Jasmine's voice was almost pleading.

"OK. I guess it doesn't hurt to just look," Trinity said.

Jasmine immediately grabbed the phone and dialed. Trinity didn't know which agent she called, but the person was more than happy to show them the place whenever they were ready. In fact, she offered to do it right then, but Jasmine told her she'd prefer to wait until the next day.

The rest of the afternoon went by with them looking at merchandise they'd love to have, and planning colors for just-in-case, as Jasmine liked to put it.

Jasmine also managed to get a lot of information out of Trinity about Drew. She seemed to keep spilling her guts, which was a habit she needed to break. She could feel a strong friendship developing between the two of them, though. She was afraid of liking Jasmine too much. She was Drew's in-law, and she and Drew were nowhere near a compromise yet.

"I'd love to stay all night, but I have to get home and sleep or I won't be any good at all tomorrow," Trinity said with reluctance. They'd stayed in the library talking for hours, and it was getting late.

"I hate for you to leave, but I understand how much more rest you need right now. I'll pick you up at noon tomorrow so we can go see the building. We'll have lunch, too. It will be great."

Jasmine went and told Drew that Trinity was ready to leave, and he was there within minutes. Trinity had to grant that he was prompt, at the very least.

Jasmine and Trinity hugged goodbye, then Drew led her to his car. As soon as she sat back in the comfortable leather, her head hit the headrest and she fell asleep.

CHAPTER SIXTEEN

I T HAD BEEN three days since she'd looked at the building with Jasmine.

Perfect.

There was no other word to describe the space they'd wandered through. Trinity had tuned out the Realtor as she ran her fingers along the window molding. It certainly needed work, and a lot of cosmetic touches, but the heart of the building was exactly what she'd always pictured.

It was even in a safe part of town with a huge parking area. She almost wished she'd never looked at it, because she wanted it more than ever.

The "girls" had talked numbers at lunch, and just the thought of the amount of money it would take to get started caused Trinity to break out in a cold sweat. She knew Jasmine could afford to foot the entire purchase, but she wanted to feel as if she were an equal partner.

She'd been trying for days to figure out a way to make it happen. The building she was in currently was rented, with an almost ridiculously high payment, so by taking on a partner, and having a mortgage instead of a rent payment, she could actually save money.

There was a good possibility that she'd also be able to make more if she had more merchandise, and the better location. She was waiting to hear back from the bank, praying they would say yes to a loan. Neither the bank nor Jasmine had called, yet. Trinity was sure the stress wasn't good for her pregnancy, but Jasmine had dangled the bait and she really wanted to bite.

Trinity knew she should get back to work, but she couldn't force herself to move. She just sat at the counter, hoping no one would come in as she thought about Drew. He seemed to be around almost every waking moment, and the more he was around, the harder it was for her to keep her distance. She might be able to do better if it weren't for the constant touching. He wouldn't go half an hour without brushing against her, or his hand sliding through her hair.

With his constant presence and touching, her body had awakened, and she felt as if she were going to die if she didn't get relief soon. How bad could it really be to sleep with him again? She could stay unattached, couldn't she? Everyone needed sex at some point, so at least it would be with the father of the child she already carried.

OK, she couldn't deny it — she was trying to justify a romp in the sack. And she'd just about talked herself into it.

He was just so attractive, and what made the ache even worse was that she remembered how his hands felt caressing her naked body. Lack of release was making her incredibly moody, causing her to snap at him often. Yet he was even a good sport about her rudeness — that was almost sickening!

He was too perfect to be real.

"Hello, beautiful; how are you feeling today?" Drew asked as he walked in and snapped her away from her thoughts.

Her face split into a smile at the sight of him. No, no, this wouldn't do. She quickly pushed it away and tried to scowl instead.

"Don't you have a business to run?" She was trying to sound stern, but failing miserably.

"The nice thing about being the boss is that I can take off whenever I want." Then he came over and kissed her on the lips.

He did that too often, as well, but she'd given up telling him no. Who was she fooling anyway? She wanted his kiss — and so much more.

Trinity fluttered her eyes shyly. "I have a doctor's appointment today. If you'd like to come along…"

Drew brightened measurably. "I'd love to."

"I'll be closing early, so if you want to be back here around two, we can go together."

"I have nothing going on today, so I'll stay here." He sat down and pulled out his laptop.

"If you insist, Drew," she told him. Yeah, right. Real reluctance!

She tried to pretend he wasn't there, but she knew the definition of insanity and she wasn't insane, so she wasn't surprised that the same thing happened that always happened. She kept sending glances his way, and her divided attention caused her to have to redo her arrangements. After about an hour, she was ready for a break.

The further along she got in her pregnancy, the harder it was for her to stand for long periods of time. If she stayed on her feet too long, her back started killing her. But she wanted to finish her bouquet, so she paused and tried to reach around and rub the aching spot.

Before she could stop him, Drew wrapped his arms around her, and he carried her to the couch. She was going to protest, but without saying a word, he sat next to her and started rubbing the sore muscles in her back. She had to fight to keep a groan from escaping. What he was doing was pure heaven.

"I should be working," she tried to protest, but not with any real effort.

"You need to take better care of yourself. It's obvious you're hurting," he countered while continuing with the back rub.

She leaned forward so he could reach lower and stopped complaining. When a few minutes later the bell on her door rang, she felt like growling at the person who dared to interrupt.

The customer picked out a couple of premade arrangements and was soon on his way. The bell rang again as a young girl walked in.

"May I help you?" Trinity asked. The moment with Drew was gone, so she might as well get back to work. She just hoped he performed his magic again later.

"I just graduated from a floral design school and would like to apply for a job," the girl said with a shy smile.

Trinity spoke with her for several minutes and liked her. She was eager and excited and, most importantly, willing to learn. Trinity took her into the back, where the girl demonstrated some of her techniques. She had a good eye for colors.

"I was planning to wait another month before hiring anyone, but you've come in at a great time, because my back is hurting more than usual," Trinity said. She hired the girl on the spot and told her to come back the next day.

"Thank you so much," she replied excitedly before rushing out the door.

"I'm glad you decided to take on an employee," Drew said.

Now that irritated her. It wasn't his business how much she worked — or didn't work. Refusing to respond to his comment, she got back to work and waited until it was time to leave for the doctor's office.

When he helped her into his luxury car, she felt like yelling in frustration, because she loved how well he was taking care of her. She was getting used to it, darn it. When he left her for someone else, as he would inevitably do, she'd miss him. She was already forgetting what it was like without him around.

As if he knew it wasn't a good time to pressure her, he said nothing as they made their way to the doctor's office.

When the doctor came into the examining room, Drew introduced himself.

"I'll bet you're eager to hear the heartbeat," the doctor said.

"I am," Drew replied. "Oh, yes, I am indeed."

As the sound of their child's heartbeat filled the room, Trinity was fixated on his face. He had such a look of wonder in his expression that tears sprung to her eyes.

"Can we do that picture thing?" Drew asked.

"She had an ultrasound a couple of months ago and everything checked out," the doctor said. "Normally, we only order another one if it looks like something's wrong. They aren't covered by insurance otherwise."

"I don't care what the cost is. I want to have it done," Drew said. The doctor agreed and sent them to a different room.

"Drew, I can't afford another ultrasound."

"I'm taking care of the baby's expenses," Drew told her, and his tone said the issue wasn't up for debate.

She didn't have insurance and had been struggling to pay for the whole thing, but she didn't appreciate his taking control in this high-handed manner.

Still, she had to be reasonable. "You don't need to take care of everything, but if you want another ultrasound, then you can take care of that."

"I'm in too good of a mood to argue, so we'll leave that

discussion for another time," he said.

She lay down on the table and glowered at him until an ultrasound technician came in and began rubbing cold goo on her stomach.

"Have you seen one of our three-dimensional ultrasounds before?"

"I had one done a couple of months ago," Trinity replied.

"I saw the picture, but I wasn't here when it was done," Drew said as he stared at the screen, his eyes riveted to the image in front of him.

The baby soon came into a clear view and Trinity turned her eyes from the screen to Drew and back. The baby was moving around, giving them several angles to look at. She was gorgeous, of course.

"Your daughter is healthy and active. Do you want to take home some more pictures?" the technician asked.

"Yes, please," Drew broke in before Trinity had a chance to answer.

"It sounds as if your husband's excited to be a father. This must be your first child."

"I can't believe she'll be here in a few short months," Drew said.

Trinity remained silent. She wasn't going to bother correcting the woman. Besides, she found it pretty amazing that he was so pumped up about being a dad.

The technician printed off a few pictures and sent them both back to the doctor's office.

"The baby is healthy, and everything is right on schedule, but you're not doing as well. Your blood pressure is too high for my liking, and that puts you at risk for getting toxemia. I need to put you on bed rest for at least two weeks; then we can reassess. You also need to eat more, because you're feeding the baby well, but you're not doing the same for yourself. You actually lost a pound this week, which shouldn't be happening at this stage in the pregnancy."

"I have to work," she argued.

"If you don't take my advice, you're risking yourself, and your baby. You could go into early labor. The chance of survival for the fetus outside the womb is below fifty percent at this point in your pregnancy," he said sternly.

"She'll go on bed rest, Doctor," Drew said and looked at her.

She wasn't happy with him, or with the doctor, at that point, but she wouldn't let her own temper harm her child. She'd just have to close the shop for a couple weeks. She couldn't imagine what that was going to do to her income.

They walked from the doctor's office in silence. On the ride to a restaurant, she sat in the seat and brooded. Once inside she ordered, but then she picked at her food. She was too upset to eat much.

"The doctor said you needed more calories, Trinity. Please eat for the baby's sake," he pleaded with her.

She forced herself to eat more, though she had a hard time getting it down her throat.

"Stop looking at me that way, Drew," she finally said. "I can't help this. I'm going to have to close the shop, and that stresses me out."

"Stress isn't good for your condition. You need to let me help you," he commanded.

"Have you considered that your tone of voice is doing nothing to alleviate my stress? And do you think I'm stupid? I know stress isn't good, Drew. I was actually listening to the freaking doctor. Also, I don't need your help. Just talking to you now is stressing me out."

"I'll call a temp agency and get someone to work at the shop.

Plus, now you have the new employee you just hired. I'll pay both their wages. You can quit shaking your head. You can't be worried about how to pay them. I'm also going to stay with you for now to make sure you're taking better care of yourself," he said.

Just great. She continued to argue with him, but she might as well have been speaking to a brick wall, because he wasn't listening.

* * *

Drew couldn't believe how much she was still fighting him each step of the way. He'd been patient, understanding, and helpful. He was trying to give her space to make the right choice, but her health was in jeopardy, and that's where he drew the line. If she wouldn't listen to him, he'd force her to.

As they stepped into her tiny apartment, he decided he was going to start searching for a new place. He couldn't stand to stay in the claustrophobic apartment for too long. His child needed more space, anyway, something with a real yard. OK, so maybe the kid could do without a real yard for a while, but he sure as hell couldn't.

Trinity immediately went to take a nap while he searched the Web for homes. He found a couple of prospective places not far from where Drew and Jasmine lived, and he made appointments for that evening. After checking on Trinity, he left to go see them.

Drew got lucky with the first house he looked at. It was practically next door to Derek, and empty. The sellers were eager to accept an offer. He could close within a week. Ten acres of property stretched out before him, leaving plenty of room for a playground, and any other thing his daughter needed. He knew Trinity would love it once she got on board with the idea of living with him. His first step was to get her in the house — then he'd get her to be his wife.

He made a cash offer that the real estate agent was sure would be accepted. Now, all he had to do was wait for the phone call. He drove back to Trinity's apartment feeling pretty good.

He let himself in with the key he'd taken and looked in on her while she was still sleeping. She must have been too warm, because she had kicked the covers off and was lying there in her tiny tank top and shorts. His body tightened with need, and it took everything he had not to join her on the bed and remind her how good they were together.

He wanted to test the weight of her curvier body while running his tongue along her most sensitive areas. He wanted her so badly, he didn't think he could take it much longer. He groaned low in his throat and headed to her tiny bathroom for an ice-cold shower.

It didn't help.

Drew tried to work in her small kitchen, but he couldn't concentrate. He hadn't slept well since the day he'd found out she was pregnant, and his eyes were trying to close on him. But when he looked at her couch, he could hardly be enthusiastic — even if it had been new, it just wasn't built for a man his size. What to do, what to do? He peeked back in on her and she was still sound asleep. Damn the consequences, he decided, and he climbed in next to her.

Trinity immediately snuggled up next to him after he lay down. She might be fighting her attraction for him while awake, but her unconscious body was clearly seeking him out. He wrapped her in his arms and fell into his first restful sleep in weeks.

CHAPTER SEVENTEEN

THE MORNING SUNLIGHT bounced off the window pane, hitting Trinity squarely in the face. She tried to turn away, and smacked into something hard. Her eyes cracked open and her gaze settled on Drew, who had his arm and leg pinning her down. Her lids shot open as she turned her head and tried to assess the situation. What had she done? How had they ended up in her bed together? She thought back to the night before and clearly remembered going to bed on her own.

OK, OK. Were they clothed? Time for a quick assessment. Whew! Yes, they were indeed dressed. Why wasn't she happier about it?

Her thoughts really started to go south at that point. Maybe she should just go for it and turn into his embrace, get relief for her aching body...

But panic set in. Wouldn't taking that step again trap her to him? And that could destroy her.

She stirred, trying to get out from beneath him without waking him up, but his arms might as well have been iron shackles. He wasn't budging.

"Mmm," he mumbled, and his hands began moving over her curves.

She sucked in her breath as his fingers caressed her back and over her backside. Her body caught on faster than her mind and she arched into him, frustration immediately setting in when her stomach got in the way of her getting closer. Pressure was building in her core, and she was quickly forgetting her reasons for not climbing on top of him.

He continued to rub along her back, then his hands switched directions and began drifting across her sides. She held her breath in agony, needing him to reach her breasts. She began to squirm; her nipples throbbed and her stomach shook. The moment he finally woke up, she felt it, because his movements took on a new urgency, his touch becoming more assured.

"We shouldn't do this," she choked out.

"We definitely should do this. Please, Trinity, I need you."

How could he say no? She couldn't. She wanted him too badly, and the complete need she heard in his voice made her feel sexy for the first time since becoming pregnant.

Suddenly, Trinity was on her back, and he was ripping away her pajamas. The look in his eyes as he took in her larger curves almost made her reach orgasm on the spot. He shed his own clothes before he bent down and kissed her with so much promise, she couldn't help but respond in kind.

He moved down her body, kissing her throat, sucking and licking the sensitive flesh. Finally, his tongue swiped across the top of her heaving breasts, while his hands continued kneading them. He circled around her incredibly sensitive peaks, teasing the corners of her nipples with his tongue, but not taking the tight bud into his mouth. She arched her back, trying to get him to do what she wanted — needed.

When she thought she couldn't take another second of this torment, his mouth clamped down, and his tongue swirled around the darkened areola. He gave one peak the attention she desired, then moved to give equal attention to the other. The building pressure, deep within her core, was unbearable, and her hips rose from the bed, seeking for him to join them as one.

He continued to play with her hardened nipples, as his hands wandered down her body. He reverently rubbed his fingers over the mound of her stomach, causing tears to well in her eyes. When his hand slid between her thighs and pushed them apart, she tensed in readiness. His fingers flicked over her sensitive flesh, and she cried out as the orgasm rocked through her.

He continued stroking her flesh as he brought his lips back up her throat. His mouth connected with hers in a tender kiss that left no doubt in her mind that she was forever his. She met him kiss for kiss, while her hands gripped his hair, needing to touch him — needing more.

She needed him to fill her. He dipped his fingers deep within her heat and she groaned as new sensations washed through her.

"Please, Drew," she cried.

He turned her onto her side, and lay down behind her, not once halting his gentle caress. His full erection pressed against her backside, and she pushed against him. His teeth nipped along her neck, while his hands massaged her breasts — lifting and pinching until she was close to shattering again.

Finally, she felt him pushing inside her, sliding into her heat, inch by beautiful inch. He began moving in and out of her slick heat, and she shook as the sensations perched her on the edge of an abyss. As if he couldn't take any more, he gripped her hip tightly in his hand, and started thrusting in and out of her. She clutched his hand to her breast, just as her body gripped his thick shaft.

His body jerked as he let out a groan, then started pumping deep within her. She joined him in plunging over the edge, her body pulsing around him. They were both drained.

No words were spoken as he rubbed her gently from her neck to her hips and back again. He let his hand drift across her stomach, sealing them as a family. She wanted to downplay the intimacy of the moment, but she couldn't. She'd never been made love to with so much passion — so much need — so much love.

"Mmm, that's the way to wake up," he whispered next to her ear, sending a shiver down her spine.

Even after the spectacular lovemaking, she wanted more. Would she never get enough?

"We probably shouldn't have done it, though, Drew." She was trying to be reasonable.

He flipped her onto her back and looked into her eyes. "You're carrying my child, and we both want each other, so what's wrong with making love?"

"I'm confused, and haven't made any decisions yet."

"It's too late for regrets," he said, and he kissed her silent once more. He showed her why there was no room for regret for half the morning. By the time they managed to crawl out of bed, Trinity was well loved and very relaxed. She would allow herself a day to satisfy her needs, without feeling guilty. Tomorrow would be soon enough for that.

Drew jumped in the shower after they ate breakfast together. Trinity knew she was supposed to be on bed rest, but she wanted to check on her shop and make sure the temp person was working out. She decided to sneak out before he got done.

She dressed quickly and left the apartment as silently as she could. She couldn't believe she felt guilty as she climbed down the stairs and started walking down the street. He didn't own her. She could go for a walk if she wanted to.

She was a few doors down from her shop when someone came up behind her, poking something into her back. She tried to move out of the way, thinking it was a person not paying attention to where he or she was going.

"Give me your purse and you won't get hurt," a man's voice growled into her ear.

Terror seized her and rendered her speechless. Shock prevented her from doing what the man asked.

"Let go. Now!" He shouted as she gripped her bag tightly to her side.

She was in the habit of wrapping the handle around her arm so she didn't drop it. Especially now, in her condition, it was too hard to bend down and pick it back up. He grabbed the strap and tugged on her bag, and she automatically pulled back.

"Are you insane, lady? Give me the bag!" he yelled. His eyes were bulging as he pulled out a knife. Her body began to shake violently, but she couldn't make her arm let go of the bag. The knife arched toward her, and she felt a stinging sensation in her arm. When she still didn't let go, he shoved her, causing her feet to slip out, and she stumbled backward, hitting the ground hard.

Pain shot up her spine, and her arm was throbbing. He took off running down the street, and her only thought was that she still had her purse. As if she were looking at herself from above, she glanced at her arm. The sight of blood streaming down made her pass out.

"Trinity, talk to me. Are you OK? Please, be OK and wake up," she heard Drew calling to her through a wall of darkness. "Please, baby, open your eyes. The ambulance is coming right now. Please, just wake up — you have to tell me where it hurts," he continued to say in a panicked voice. She couldn't understand why he was yelling. She was just trying to sleep.

"I'm tired," she finally managed to mumble, and she felt his hands roam over her body. She tried to push him away. She just wanted to sleep. He passed over her arm, and pain spiraled in all directions, immediately waking her up. Her eyes flew open, and she found herself looking into his terrified eyes. The entire event came flying back to her.

"Ouch" was what she finally managed to get past her tight throat.

"They'll be here in a few more seconds. Do you hear the sirens?"

"He tried to take my purse. I tried to let it go, but my hand wouldn't listen to my brain."

"I should have been with you. I'm so sorry, baby. I'm so sorry. If anything happens to you or our daughter, I'll never forgive myself," he moaned as he rubbed her face and head. "Tell me where it hurts," he pleaded.

"My arm and back," she told him with a grimace.

"He cut your arm, and someone said they saw him push you down. Does your stomach hurt?" he asked, terrified of what her answer would be.

"I don't know, Drew. My back hurts really badly. I can't tell if my stomach does, too," she said as tears ran down her face. "My baby!" she cried as her hands clutched her stomach.

The ambulance pulled up and the paramedics rushed forward. They asked her a few questions and placed a neck brace on her before lifting her up to the gurney.

Drew refused to leave her side. He rode next to her in the ambulance, whispering reassurances and holding her hand the whole way.

As soon as she was rushed into the emergency room, a

doctor checked on her. People hooked all kinds of monitors to her, and soon she could hear the sound of her baby's heartbeat. Both she and Drew breathed a sigh of relief at the healthy sound.

"The baby doesn't seem to be in any immediate danger, but your blood pressure is dangerously high. It shows here that you were supposed to be on bed rest, not on the streets," the doctor scolded.

"I'm sorry. It was just a small walk," she tried to explain, but she was feeling her own guilt, and she would do whatever the doctor asked, now.

"We're going to stitch up your arm. You're staying overnight so we can monitor you and the baby. If we can get your blood pressure down, then you can get released tomorrow, but only if you're on strict bed rest. That is, you go from your bed to a couch and back again. You're not to take walks; you're not to work; you're to be waited on hand and foot," the doctor continued to speak sternly.

"I understand," she said.

They poked and prodded her before she was finally moved to a private room. She breathed a sigh of relief as the pills kicked in and she drifted into blissful sleep. She couldn't understand how the day could start off so well, and end so badly.

CHAPTER EIGHTEEN

DREW MADE CALLS to his family, and he knew they'd be there in no time. His cousins would drop whatever they were doing to be there for each other. Family came first — always. This was his future wife, carrying his child, lying in a hospital bed. They would have been outraged with him if he hadn't called. The second she'd conceived his baby, she'd become a part of his tight family circle.

While Drew paced the stark hospital hallways, his phone rang. He looked in the door, saw that Trinity was still sleeping, and so took the call.

"Yes?"

"Mr. Titan, this is Bridget, from Remart Realty. The sellers accepted your offer."

"Thank you. That's perfect timing," he said. He hung up the phone, feeling a bit of relief for the first time since he'd found Trinity unconscious on the sidewalk. He was getting her out of that area, whether she liked it or not.

Drew instantly went into planning mode — what he did best. He called up his normal temp agency and had them start performing interviews for a household staff. He wanted everything ready as soon as he got the keys. As he continued pacing the hallways, he saw Derek and Ryan round the corner. They spotted him and immediately demanded information. He explained everything, and they talked him into going for some much-needed coffee.

"Don't worry, Drew," Jasmine told him. "I'll stay with Trinity. She won't wake up alone."

The three men were silent as they made their way to the large cafeteria and found a table in the corner where they could talk.

"How the hell does something like that happen in broad daylight?" Ryan slammed his mug on the table, his tension evident.

"I don't understand what kind of a scumbag would attack a pregnant woman. I want her out of there, now," Drew thundered.

"I agree with you, Drew. She's already been through a lot, though, so be careful not to push so hard she has a relapse," Derek reminded him.

"Her health is the issue. She was on orders from the doctor for bed rest, yet she still managed to sneak out. Now, she doesn't have a hell of a lot of choice but to listen to me for a while," Drew said with no little satisfaction. He knew very well how independent Trinity was trying to be. He also knew how much she already loved their child. She'd do anything in her power to keep her safe.

"I have some good news for you," Derek told him. "Jasmine and Trinity were talking about opening a business together, and Jasmine found a perfect space. We purchased it yesterday. It's not far from where we're living and in a much safer part of town. Jasmine was actually coming over today to tell her she'd snatched it up before it was gone."

"That's great, Derek. I'll feel much better if she's not living, or working, on that side of town. Plus, the women will have each other and Trinity won't be alone. I don't like her working by herself, no matter what neighborhood she's in," Drew said.

"I agree. I'm going to talk to Jasmine about having help. She plans on having the baby with her, and she'll need extra people on staff. Hell, money isn't an issue, anyway, but their safety is."

"Don't let Jasmine hear you say that. She gets really offended if you act like money's disposable," Drew said, causing Ryan to laugh.

"I'm sure glad that I don't have anyone other than you guys to stress over, because it doesn't sound like any fun," Ryan said. Both Derek and Drew turned to glare at him.

"Your time is coming," Derek finally said.

Ryan just shook his head. Was that a look of terror on his face? He was certain that he wasn't ready to head down that road.

"Not a chance," he replied.

The three of them relaxed since there was a clear plan of action in place. None of them liked feeling helpless. It brought back those years when they had nothing — when times seemed almost hopeless.

Drew wasn't looking forward to the conversation with Trinity, but then again, he was the successful businessman he was because he never backed down. He could handle any situation, including a very angry woman. He smiled in anticipation.

* * *

Jasmine sat by the bed, waiting anxiously for Trinity to

wake up. She wanted to share her news with her, but more importantly, she wanted to hear Trinity's voice — to know she was OK. If anything had happened to that child, it would destroy Trinity. Though Jasmine hadn't known her very long, she knew from her own experience as a mother how bonded you became with your child, even when it was still in the womb.

"Is she still sleeping?" a man asked as he walked in the room.

Jasmine looked at the gorgeous creature, thinking the plot had just thickened, as the man came and sat by Trinity's bed, his face clearly showing his grief.

"She hasn't stirred, yet. I'm Jasmine," she said, sticking out her hand.

"I'm Damien Whitfield, Trinity's best friend. Drew called and told me what happened," he said, taking her hand for only a brief moment. He then immediately returned his attention to Trinity.

Jasmine was relieved to hear he was a friend only. Otherwise there might have been a fight in the hospital room. Drew was a bit territorial, especially with Trinity carrying his child.

Jasmine and Damien spoke quietly while he gripped Trinity's hand. She could see he wasn't going anywhere until his friend woke and told him she was fine. Trinity was a very lucky girl to inspire such friendship, Jasmine thought.

* * *

Trinity heard whispering as she slowly gained consciousness. It took her a moment to remember where she was and for everything to come back to her. She let the sound of her friends' voices soothe her fear, then took a deep breath before she opened her eyes. Her face lit up with a smile as she turned to Damien. It didn't take either of her visitors long to realize she was awake.

"How are you doing?" they asked simultaneously, which made Trinity's smile even wider.

"I've had better days," she attempted to joke, but her voice came out too cracked to pull it off.

"I'm so sorry about what happened," Jasmine told her with tears in her eyes.

Damien sat by quietly while rubbing Trinity's hand, giving her time to gather her strength.

"It was my fault. I shouldn't have been out there in the first place. The doctor told me to stay in bed, but I was determined to check on my shop," Trinity said.

"Trinity, you're always putting too much pressure on yourself," Damien said with firm compassion. "Don't start playing the blame game, or you'll cause yourself more stress." He bent down and kissed her cheek, taking any sting out of his words with his affectionate gesture.

"I know, but the baby…" she replied in a fearful whisper.

"The baby is doing great. She's healthy, has a strong heartbeat, and is nice and cozy inside of you. If you took care of yourself as well as you take care of your child, you'd feel on top of the world, too," he insisted.

"How do you always know the exact right thing to say?"

"Because I'm irresistibly charming and handsome. Say the word, and I'll cart you away — steal you right out from under Drew," he said with a gleeful expression. His attitude helped ease her worries much better than any medicine could.

"You know I'd be too much for you to handle," Trinity told him.

Damien clutched his chest. "Ah, you break my heart, woman."

"I love you, you know," Trinity said as tears clogged her

throat.

"I love you, too. I had to make sure you were OK with my own eyes, but I'm in the middle of a huge merger and have a roomful of men sitting at a table wondering why I just ran from the room. Not that I care, and you know you'll always come first, but now that I know you'll be OK, I have to get back to the offices. I can only go if you promise to call me if anything at all changes," Damien said.

"I promise, Damien."

He bent and kissed Trinity's forehead before he quickly departed. She was grateful to have him in her life. He was always so busy with business, she didn't get to see him nearly enough anymore. Hmmm. It might be time to start doing some matchmaking for this best friend of hers. Too bad Jasmine was already married. That would have been about as perfect as could be.

"I have some great news to share with you," Jasmine said, pulling Trinity's attention away from the door Damien had just walked through. "The building we checked out had another offer on it, so Derek stepped in and gave them a figure they couldn't refuse. They accepted. The shop is ours. I know I should have waited to talk to you, but we would have lost it, and I really want to do this with you."

"That's great, Jasmine, but I haven't figured out if I can afford it yet," Trinity said with regret. "Is there any way for you and Derek to back out of the real estate deal? I don't want to cause trouble, but…" She so wanted to share a shop with Jasmine, but she refused to let Jasmine foot the entire bill.

"Don't worry about any of that right now. We'll work it out. The point is, we have the space and can spend the rest of the day getting it designed, and then Ryan can get started on remodeling," Jasmine told her.

Jasmine was so excited that Trinity couldn't help but get equally fired up. Jasmine pulled out some paper, and the two women spent the next few hours figuring out how they wanted the shop to look. They were both giggling like children as their store started to take shape on the piece of paper. Jasmine was an impressive artist. Trinity could almost see the finished product in her mind. It was real, and it was spectacular.

When the men returned, the girls shushed them and continued with their plans. They were oblivious to anything but their future shop. The men sat back, waiting impatiently, while Trinity and Jasmine simply ignored them.

"I think we have it. What do you think?" Trinity asked.

"It's perfect," Jasmine agreed as she reached over and gave Trinity a big hug. "Here you go, Ryan. The place is ready for your magic touch."

"Then magic is what you'll get," Ryan replied.

"We know it will be out of this world once you're finished," Jasmine said with confidence.

"I aim to please."

Jasmine had shown Trinity some of Ryan's portfolio and he was a true artist.

"So you prefer working on historic sites?" Trinity asked shyly. Jasmine had told her a little about what Ryan did, and Trinity was now aware that his services were greatly in demand. She was awed that even though he had unlimited work lined up, he was dropping everything for their project.

"I love working with any kind of building, but I do have a soft spot for historical places," he answered with a shrug, as if it were no big deal.

Jasmine leaned up and kissed him on the cheek. "You know you're the best guy ever, right?"

"If I keep getting rewarded like that, I'll be at your beck and call, seven days a week," he said with a wink.

He turned to Trinity and waggled his eyebrows. She laughed and wiggled her fingers for him to come closer. He leaned down and she also kissed him on the cheek.

"OK, enough of that," Drew growled, while scowling at his cousin.

"I'm irresistible," Ryan said with a shrug. Both women laughed and the other cousins glared, perhaps in part because they always said the same about themselves. Ryan continued to laugh.

"OK, everyone out. Trinity needs rest," Drew told his family.

She was actually grateful. She was falling a little in love with each one of them, but she really was exhausted.

All four Titans hugged Trinity and wished her well, then trudged out of the room. Her dinner was brought in and she ate it all, even though she made faces at the poor flavor. After she was finished, she couldn't keep her eyes open any longer and soon drifted to sleep.

CHAPTER NINETEEN

O KAY, MS. MATHEWS, I'll release you today, but only if you promise me that you won't be alone, and that you stay home."

"I promise," Trinity said. She wanted out of the hospital. She'd be willing to promise just about anything if they'd spring her from this prison.

"I'll be with her the entire time and will make sure she doesn't do anything to harm herself or our child," Drew said.

"OK then, Mr. Titan; I'm leaving her in your care," the doctor told him, as if she were a child who didn't know how to behave.

Men could be insufferable. And what if she'd been completely indigent and with no one to support her? Would the doctor have worried so much about her being alone?

He looked at them again before signing her release papers. Trinity didn't waste any time getting ready and heading for the front doors. It was bad enough that she had to be pushed out in a wheelchair though she could walk perfectly well without assistance. Stupid medical profession. She was sure the stricter bed rest was going to be even worse than she imagined. Was this patriarchal and condescending doctor a quack who knew nothing about women's health? She'd better do some research about bed rest on the Web.

As Drew drove to her apartment, he asked her if she was OK so many times that she was ready to slug him and then ask if *he* was OK. When he tried to carry her up the stairs, she put her foot down. She wasn't an invalid who couldn't walk.

Seeing the dangerous glitter in her eyes, he wisely backed off and gave her room, but of course had to make a condition: only if she took it slow. Grrrrrrr. She gritted her teeth but took her time walking slowly up the stairs.

Trinity knew the apartment was going to get crowded fast. The more Drew hovered over her, the grumpier she'd become. She didn't want to admit that to him, though. The doctor had said she couldn't be alone — and that gave him entirely too much power.

"You need to sit down and relax while I make you something to eat," Drew said in a commanding voice.

Watch out, sweetie, Trinity thought. There could be a homicide by the time her bed rest ended. If he continued to command her, she wouldn't be responsible for her actions. She sat, but not without resentment. Soon, however, the smell from the kitchen eased her grumpiness. She was starving after the criminal hospital food. Those people obviously wanted repeat customers!

He handed her a plate and she took her first bite. Oh, my. Now this was food. It had flavor. It had texture. She could eat this.

Her words to him were more restrained than the reaction of her taste buds. "This is good. Thank you, Drew."

"Trinity, I need to talk to you."

Huh? She'd just started eating and he broke in like that? She stared at him. So what on earth was wrong?

"Go ahead and spit it out," she said, worried by his tone.

"I bought a new home. It's close to Derek and Jasmine."

"That's great. You must be excited. You know you don't have to stay here and babysit me if you want to get settled in."

"I bought the place for us," he said, maintaining eye contact.

A lot of thoughts ran through her head. Why was one of them a desire to just agree? That flummoxed her But...it would be nice to live with him, to be a real family, to...

Before she could think like that, she cleared her head and reminded herself of her goals, her plans, and the fact that she'd vowed not to "do relationships" anymore.

"I...you...we aren't a couple," she finally sputtered.

"Trinity, we *are* a couple. We're sexually compatible. We enjoy being together, and to top that off, we're having a child. We *will* get married, but I'm willing to give you more time to get used to the idea."

He thinks he's being so magnanimous. Trinity just looked at him.

Her look didn't stop him. "But you *are* on strict doctor's orders not to be alone and to stay in bed. This place is too small for us to remain comfortable, so it makes sense for you to move in with me."

"I'm fine in my own place," she said, as she crossed her arms over her chest.

"Look, I don't want to be a jerk, Trinity, but you're not safe here, which means my child isn't safe. Are you so selfish that you'd endanger our child for the sake of your pride?"

Trinity looked at Drew in shock. That was a low blow. How dare he imply she didn't have her child's best interest in mind at all times?

"I love my child, Drew."

"I know you do, Trinity, and that was a crappy thing to say. I'm sorry. How about a compromise? You're going to be on bed rest for a while," he said. "Stay with me until after the baby is born so I can help take care of you. If we haven't managed to work things out by then, we can reassess our situation. You know this apartment is too small for a baby, anyway."

She was grateful when he gave her a few minutes to think. What if she moved in, fell hopelessly in love, and then had to leave? She'd never be the same again. He was already a part of her life through their daughter. What would happen when she couldn't do anything without the child reminding her of him?

"I don't think I'm ready for this, Drew." That's what she said, but she was beginning to cave. She was fighting herself as much as him.

"Trinity, darling, I can't stay in this place. It would drive me insane. So you can either move into the large house with me, where you'll be waited on and pampered...or I'll move in there, and you'll have to go back to the hospital, because the doctor said you weren't to be alone." He had too much confidence in his voice, and then he sat back with a smug look on his face. He knew he'd just achieved checkmate.

He didn't want to be a jerk? Give her a break! She glared at him for several minutes, trying to break him down, but she knew he was well aware of how badly she hated that hospital. He was blackmailing her, plain and simple. She'd much rather be anywhere other than that sterile hospital room. She was considering it, though, just so he couldn't have his way, but then she'd only be punishing herself.

"Fine, Drew. I guess I'll move in, but when I'm better, we'll talk about this again."

He threw his arms around her and then grabbed the laptop so she could see photos and a detailed description of the house.

She didn't want to admit it, but she was impressed with his taste. It was beautiful, and so much larger than anything she was used to. If she gave in, she was afraid it would be hard to go back to a normal life again. Drew was bigger than life, and everything he did reflected that.

The next few weeks crept by with the two of them crammed together in her place. Trinity was getting closer to that homicide every day. Drew was everywhere, all the time, and the more she was around him, the harder it was to remember her reasons for not being romantically involved. Not being able to go outside was also making her edgy. He promised her he'd set up a lounge on the deck at the new place so she could at least get fresh air.

She sat and watched him pack the last of her items, feeling self-conscious as he went through everything she owned. At least he approached it as she was sure he approached business, methodically and in a no-nonsense fashion. He even labeled each box before moving to the next.

"I never thought there'd be a day I'd be happy to pack boxes, but at least it gives me something to do other than twiddle my thumbs. I have to tell you, your apartment is driving me crazy," he muttered as he finished another box.

"You can leave any time you want," she snapped.

"I'm dealing with it, and it's only for one more day," he said, choosing to ignore her bad attitude. "I called the Salvation Army and they'll be here early in the morning to pick up the furniture we aren't keeping," he finished.

"*We* aren't keeping? *I* happen to think that it's perfectly fine furniture, and I don't see why we can't use it," she snapped again. Her feet were swollen, even bigger than before, and her place didn't have air conditioning. She was ready to bite anyone's head off. Drew just happened to be the only person around.

"I'm not trying to put your furniture down, Trinity, and

you know it. But, come on. Nothing matches and a few of the pieces have duct tape holding them together," he said with more patience than she deserved. OK, no patience at all.

She wasn't going to fight him too hard on the matter, because she'd bought the furniture secondhand, at an excellent price, and was sure she could pick up more if she needed it. It was simply a matter of her pride. She thought she'd done well with her apartment, especially considering the budget she had. Now she'd be living in a billionaire's mega-mansion, and for now, at least, the word *budget* seemed almost laughable.

CHAPTER TWENTY

Y OU KNOW I'M not going to be a kept woman, don't you? Just because we made a child together doesn't mean you're going to take over my life."

Drew grinned, not even trying to hide his amusement. He found her ill-temper charming. He also loved how independent she was, and how she wasn't afraid to call him on his arrogance. There were too many people afraid to talk back to him. He wouldn't be falling in love with her if she were like the majority of the other people in his life. Hell, not just the majority — virtually everyone else apart from family and a few close friends.

"I'd never think of you as a kept woman," he finally managed to say without bursting into laughter. He must not have been doing a good enough job, because her glare grew even more deadly.

When he turned away and started on another box, he heard her grumble something or other, but he chose to ignore it. She'd been trying to pick a fight with him for two days, and he was surprised that he wasn't angered by it. He knew they'd both feel better when they got into the new place and had more space. It would also be helpful to have Jasmine visit so the women could do the girl-talk thing.

Drew had no idea how lucky he was that Trinity couldn't read all his thoughts.

"We're moving right along, Trinity. I think it's time to start packing your clothes."

Her cheeks turned pink, and he immediately wanted to know what she was embarrassed about having him see. He figured a good place to start would be her panty drawer.

"I can do that on my own," she grumbled.

"The doctor said complete bed rest, so you can lie in bed and direct me," he told her with a wicked grin and a waggle of his brows.

She blushed and looked away. "You can help me with my closet, but I'll take care of the dresser," she finally said with an unutterably grim look.

Generous as always, he'd give her that one, so he shrugged his shoulders and followed her into the bedroom.

Drew couldn't help glancing back at Trinity as she lay on the bed and closed her eyes. She fought sleep but eventually lost the battle. Drew tucked the light blanket around her and gently kissed her on the forehead, then left the room so she could nap in peace.

The moving company was arriving in the morning, and most of the house was already packed, so Drew went into town for a while.

He called his cousins and the three met at a local furniture store that somehow managed to do right by billionaires. The men quickly picked out a basic selection of furniture so the home could be comfortable their first night in it. What surprised Drew was the way he enjoyed himself as he did it. He never thought he'd be the settling-down kind of guy, but being with Trinity was sure changing his perspective on life.

As the men walked into the baby's section, and he gazed around at the tiny furniture, he realized he was completely clueless. He had no idea what to buy for his new daughter.

"Why does a baby need such a massive amount of stuff?"

"I don't know, but I think Britney has more furniture than we do. Jasmine says all of it is vital, but I honestly couldn't tell you why. Look at this thing, for example. It's a changing table, but I've never used it. We always bring her in our room and just change her on the bed," Derek said, looking just as perplexed as Drew.

"We need help," Ryan piped up.

Derek called Jasmine, who was more than happy to rush down to the store and help them. Within an hour of her arrival, they had a fully stocked nursery. Drew also got serious lessons in what to do and not to do as far as decorating went.

As they finished paying and got ready to leave, Drew looked down at the crib, picturing his tiny daughter asleep inside, and found himself fighting a surge of emotions. He couldn't believe that in a short amount of time, he would be a father. It was happening so quickly. The doctor didn't think she'd make the full forty weeks. He was hoping for her to make it to at least thirty-six.

Once they all got outside, Drew turned to his cousins and to Jasmine. "Thanks for the help." He hoped that he wasn't blushing. Men didn't blush.

"Any time — you know that," Derek said. "We need to get together this weekend. I'm taking the next two weeks off from the office."

"I'll take it off, too," Ryan agreed. "What are billions for?"

"Good. Perfect timing for you guys to help me get the house

together. Kind of like a barn raising."

Ryan and Derek groaned as they realized the trap they'd set for themselves. They nodded good-naturedly before the three men went their separate ways.

Drew headed back to the apartment bearing an arsenal of takeout boxes, and when he walked through the door, Trinity was just starting to wake up. Rubbing her eyes groggily, she walked into the living room.

"Something smells good, Drew."

"I tried that new barbecue place a couple of miles away," Drew said as he began to draw cartons out of a large paper bag. "I wanted Chinese badly, but you're still on a low-sodium diet."

"I can't wait for this child to be born,so I can go back to eating like a normal person. I'm hungry all the time, and limited on what I get to have."

"According to the doctor, you're not eating enough," he hastened to remind her as he piled her plate with food.

After she'd finished only about a quarter of her dinner, she pushed the plate away.

Damn, she was irritating him. She needed to take better care of her own needs, which meant she had to eat more. Drew pushed the plate back toward her but she ignored him. He gave up for the moment and pondered his strategy. He'd get her to eat more later; after all, she normally got hungry in the middle of the night. And when she got hungry, get back!

After dinner, Trinity went back to bed and Drew cleaned up their dinner mess. As he took a shower, he had to smile when he thought about how nice it was to have her by his side every night. Even with her mood swings, and with her constant attempts to fight with him, he still looked forward to every moment.

He used to think marriage and kids would be the same as a

death sentence. Now, he had no idea why he'd fought so hard against it.

When he crawled in bed, she stopped tossing at once as she snuggled into him and fell into a restful sleep. As he lay down next to her, his body came alive, as always. Damn. Damn. Damn. If the doctor didn't give her a go-ahead to resume normal activity at her next visit, he probably wouldn't make it alive to see his daughter's birth.

* * *

Drew and Trinity woke up late the next morning, and they were rushing around to finish the last-minute details before the movers arrived. She had Drew gather her toiletries while she did a final search of her cupboards and drawers. In a way her paranoia was silly. She'd lived in so many different places in her life, and she was always afraid during every hateful move that she'd leave something behind whenever she had to move on. And yet, when she came down to it, the things she'd been worried about weren't all that worth protecting. And so, when the Salvation Army workers showed up and carted off her old furniture, she was a little sad. It wasn't much, but she'd worked hard for everything she had, and she'd valued it that much more because of her struggles. And now she was wandering off with a billionaire. Sheesh.

When the men thanked her for her donation and left, she was left with a barren apartment, nothing inside but a pile of boxes. And those were soon gone. The moving company showed up within minutes, and her apartment was cleared out within an hour. Drew sent the movers ahead of them, and she gathered up her purse and followed him out the door. With the keys now in the apartment manager's hand, she walked out of the place she had called home for the past couple of years. And what was really sad? That she wasn't that sad at all. When it came down to it, she wasn't upset to leave, not after dealing with the crowded space and stifling heat of the last few weeks.

Drew helped her into his car, and they were off to the new house. Her heart was palpitating. She'd only seen pictures of the new home online, and she was looking forward to actually seeing it in person.

The drive took only about twenty minutes. Twenty minutes to a new life. And then they were entering a locked gate and making their way down a winding driveway. As they turned the last bend, she got her first view of the house, and her eyes widened in delight. It was certainly large, but it had a wraparound front porch with a swing already in place. This house could actually turn into a home.

Trinity stepped inside, careful to stay out of the movers' way as she looked around at all the possibilities before her. There was so much space to fill. Scattered pieces of furniture adorned the rooms, but the house looked empty. She could picture the walls done in pastel colors, with framed photos lining the hall.

She'd never had the money to decorate the way she wanted to. But an idea rose up in her eager imagination: even if she wasn't there a long time, it would be her gift to him to decorate the place beautifully. She knew she had a great eye; that was why she'd chosen to be a florist. Creating a bouquet for someone's special day was a form of art.

She wandered from room to room, gasping in delight at each new space she found. There was even a library, similar to the one at Jasmine's house. Sure, it was a bit much to have such a large home — so many thousands of feet for just the two of them and the baby? — she was delighted with it. Her early reservations were melting away.

She stepped through the French doors and was delighted to find an outdoor kitchen. She'd always fantasized about having one. She could imagine her daughter playing in the swimming pool while she cooked dinner. Then they'd all eat beneath the stars. Dang. It wouldn't be easy to go back to an apartment after living in a mansion like this one.

"I want to show you something, and remember that if you don't like any of it, we can return it and get what you want. But I wanted to help you since you're on bed rest," he told her as they slowly made their way up the beautiful staircase.

He opened a door, and she felt tears fall as her feet drew her into the room. It was fully stocked with baby furniture. He'd thought of everything. She walked over to the gorgeous canopied bed and looked inside, excited for the day her daughter would lay her little head there.

Drew's apprehension was clear. "I didn't pick out any of the bedding or anything because Jasmine said you'd want to choose your own theme, but she said you should like this cherry wood."

Trinity walked up to him and wrapped him in her arms, as much as her large belly would allow. "Thank you, Drew. It's all perfect," she said with a sniffle. The more things he did, the more she realized how hard it would be to let him go.

A beautiful changing table and matching dresser sat between a door that led to a walk-in closet. She didn't understand the need for one in a baby's room, but she was sure he'd want to fill the shelves to overflowing. Trinity had no doubt that Drew would spoil their daughter shamelessly. The words *deadbeat dad* didn't belong on the same planet with him.

Once Trinity spotted the glider rocking chair — it looked so comfortable! — she lost focus on everything else. She walked over and sank deep into the cushions with a long sigh. Her eyelids grew heavy as the day's events caught up to her. She'd just rest for a few moments.

Drew pushed a button on the rocker and part of the base rose to cushion her swollen feet. Its back reclined at the same time, and she knew she was going to pass out within moments...

* * *

Drew was home — right where he was supposed to be. As Trinity drifted off to sleep and he surveyed the room his daughter would soon occupy, he knew his life would never be the same. They were a family and he'd do anything to keep them together. He wouldn't ever let her go, and he didn't care how long it took to convince her. He'd just make her life too appealing for her to want to leave.

Yes, he'd lied to her at the beginning of their relationship, but they'd come a long way since then. She'd soon realize she could trust him where it mattered most. Maybe he'd earn her trust when she realized that he'd put the house in her name, and that he wanted nothing more than her love.

Drew walked over and picked up the blanket he had waiting for her, tucked it gently around her shoulders, and then leaned forward and softly kissed her cheek. She murmured in her sleep, then snuggled deeper into the chair. After one last glance, he turned and walked from the room.

Derek and Ryan would be arriving any minute, and they had a lot to get done. When Trinity woke up, he wanted her to find the boxes gone and the house looking more like a home. Home — he was finally home.

CHAPTER TWENTY-ONE

T HIS PLACE IS beautiful, Trinity," Jasmine exclaimed as they walked from the front door into the main house. "I'm at your beck and call to fill up that library."

"It's pretty great, but this is only temporary, so I don't want to add too much right now," Trinity said. Caution was one of her middle names.

"I'd love to go through those catalogs with you if you need help. We need to get you tucked up on the couch before your warden finds out you're on your feet," Jasmine said.

Trinity knew Jasmine was kidding, but she wasn't far off the truth. Drew seemed to have a radar go off anytime she got up for longer than a few seconds. She was thinking this bed rest stuff was going to raise her blood pressure far more than taking a simple walk would. She'd really have to do her Web research on bed rest.

"I'd appreciate it. It's all a little overwhelming, but since I can't go anywhere or do anything physical right now, it's kind of nice having something to keep me occupied."

The two women sat down and soon racked up the charges

on Drew's credit card. Trinity wouldn't have ordered even half of what she did if Jasmine hadn't insisted. Plus, Trinity was irritated with Drew for being such a prison guard. She hoped to irritate him a bit with the spending, even if it was on his own house…er…mansion…er…palace.

"These boys have enough money to feed a small country. He'll be fine," Jasmine said.

Double damn. Trinity had a feeling that Drew wasn't going to notice the dent she'd made in his bank account, and that took some of the pleasure out of her tantrum. The baby items were her favorite things to order, and she couldn't wait for them to be delivered. When the shipment came in, the nursery would be finished and waiting for their daughter.

The cook brought in lunch and they ate while continuing through the many catalogs. Once they were finished with the home decor, Jasmine pulled out a bag with a handful of other catalogs.

"Ryan is halfway finished with the remodel work on our shop, so now comes the fun part. We can begin ordering supplies and merchandise. I think I brought everything you'll need to set up the floral department. This company will bring the coolers out and set them up. It's a bigger space, so you'll have more display area. I also found a great company for gift items. I know my portion is supposed to be the café, but I'd love to help with the gift section, too."

"I've always wanted to have a bigger shop, Jasmine, but I'm in the dark with what needs to be done, so I'm more than happy you want to be a part of it."

Once the women became immersed in the catalogs, time slipped away. Each new purchase made their business venture that much more real, and their excitement grew.

Drew and Derek came in a couple of times, but they left

quickly. They hardly wanted to get suckered into looking at the mountains of prospective purchases that the women thought were so great.

Jasmine had been right — Drew didn't care a bit about what they were spending. He hadn't even blinked when Trinity had shown him what she'd ordered. She couldn't possibly think of what she could do to get under his skin.

But she had to worry. Unlike Drew and his family, Trinity just wasn't used to flinging money around like this. And when she figured out how much money she and Jasmine had blown in one afternoon, she couldn't help but worry. What if the business failed? What if she failed?

But Jasmine reassured her that their location was phenomenal, and she insisted that they'd sell out in no time. Even that was great for her because then they'd get to place even more orders!

By the time the baby arrived, everything would be ready to go, and she'd be able to enjoy working again. One great thing about being a business owner was that she could take her daughter with her. There was no way she wanted a stranger to raise her child while she worked all day.

The best thing? Their two daughters would have the chance to grow up together and become close. That was one thing she really wished she had — family. Ryan was creating a spectacular play area, which would benefit their daughters and their clients' children as well.

The day slipped away and before she knew it, Trinity was saying goodbye. It hit her that she was all alone with Drew for the first time that day. What would happen in the night ahead? They'd never discussed sleeping arrangements, and just thinking about them made her jumpy.

OK, they hadn't talked about it when they were in her

apartment, either. He'd just started sleeping each night with her, which was understandable because it was either that or on a very uncomfortable couch. But they had a huge house to share now, so she wasn't sure what he wanted to do. And for that matter, she hadn't a clue about what she really wanted. Or did she?

Drew led her up the stairs and opened the doors to the master bedroom. She was delighted to find that his cousins had been busy while she and Jasmine had been lounging in the library and spending money.

Trinity couldn't suppress her awe. "Wow, Drew. This room is spectacular." She stepped into the huge closet and noticed it was filled with both of their clothes. With a deep breath of courage, she added, "I don't think it's a great idea for us to share a room."

Drew deliberately wrapped his arms around her and looked into her eyes. "I know things haven't been perfect, and I've kind of bullied you into this situation, but we've been sleeping in the same bed every night for the last couple weeks. I won't pressure you into sex before you're ready, especially because it's forbidden in strict bed rest, but I'm not budging on the sleeping arrangements," he said. The words were spoken with steel, but his hands were gentle while wrapped around her body.

She was tempted to kick him in the shins and march to another room, just because he was once again telling her what to do.

"I knew you'd try and fight me on this," he said with a disgustingly smug smile. "And that's why there are no other beds in the house."

Her look was murderous. There were a few comfortable couches she could sleep on, and she was seriously contemplating doing just that.

"Oh, come on, Trinity. It's not that bad to share a bed with me."

"Fine, I'll sleep in here for tonight because I'm exhausted, but I'm not snuggling with you," she snapped. She knew she sounded like a pouting child, but the guy always seemed to get his way and it was frustrating. He shrugged as if it didn't matter, then started stripping his clothes away.

Trinity couldn't breathe when he stood before her in nothing but his boxer shorts. The man was so incredibly sexy, standing before her with his Adonis chest and ripped abs. As her gaze continued down his body, her breath caught at the site of his arousal stretching the front of his boxers. When her eyes snapped back to his face, he smiled wickedly.

"All you have to do is ask, and we could both go to sleep feeling…happy," he told her.

She was sorely tempted to take him up on his offer. She wanted him, and just looking at his beautiful body sent her pulse through the roof and heat flowing to her core. She didn't understand how he could possibly want her. Pregnancy was supposed to be beautiful, but she felt more like a whale.

As she teetered on the edge, not knowing what to do, Drew stepped forward and touched his lips to hers in a tender kiss. Nothing on their bodies touched, until she felt herself swaying into him. Her stubborn mind might be saying no, but her alert body knew exactly what it wanted. She couldn't resist him when he caressed her so gently. He ran his tongue along her lips and gently nipped her mouth. She moaned at the pleasure of his touch, opening her mouth for him to slip inside. He caressed her mouth, and she quivered with need. Slipping in and out of her mouth, his tongue mimicked what she wanted their bodies to be doing.

He finally ran his hands up her sides and slipped them under her shirt, caressing her rounded stomach first, and then reaching her swollen breasts. Her nipples were peaked in anticipation of his touch. When he brushed his palms over the hard tips, her entire body jerked with pleasure and passion.

He broke the kiss long enough to pull her shirt over her head, then brought their lips back together again. He moved slowly, and she knew she could stop the seduction at any time. The power of that knowledge nearly brought her to her knees. He was leaving their lovemaking up to her, but his powers of seduction made him impossible to resist. And earthquake couldn't have stopped her from reaching for him. She needed to be loved in a way that only he could offer.

He changed his slow caresses to urgent, desired-filled kisses. His hands roamed every inch of her skin. Her knees began shaking and she knew she wouldn't be able to stand much longer. Before she could fall, Drew scooped her into his arms and laid her on the bed without breaking the kiss. She sighed in pleasure as his hands swept down her body and he spread her legs.

"Tell me you want me, and you won't have regrets," he said.

She didn't want to say the words. It was too much like giving in. When she didn't respond, he pulled back from her aching heat to look at her face. She cried out in agony and desperation. He rubbed her thighs and circled her core, making her whimper.

"Tell me you want me to touch you, Trinity," he growled as he continued to touch her everywhere but the one spot where she wanted it most.

"Please, Drew. I need you," she gasped.

He opened her fully to his view, then dipped his head, and swiped his tongue across her swollen bundle of nerves, her center of pleasure and desire. She had no fight left and she cried out as he inserted his fingers into her dripping heat. Her body convulsed and lifted off the bed as he continued to stroke her hot flesh with his tongue.

"Please, Drew. I need you inside me," she cried.

He continued to stroke her with his tongue, mercilessly. When he sucked her swollen bud into his mouth, she soared higher than ever before. He slowly continued stroking her flesh. He was driving her crazy. When her shaking started to recede, he turned her body, kissing his way up her hips and waist and then beyond. He sucked on her neck, making the heat and the tension inside her begin to build again. He brought his hands around to her breasts and rubbed them, and then pinched her nipples between his fingers. He soothed the light sting by rubbing the thumb of one hand across the spot that he'd just tormented, bringing only pleasure.

He let his other hand drift below her stomach, and he reached the apex of her thighs, as he opened her up and began pushing slowly inside. She pushed against him, needing him all, every glorious inch. Each time she was with him, her need only grew greater. She couldn't seem to get enough.

"No regrets," he demanded. With only half his length inside her, he'd stopped, and no matter how much she pushed against him, he wouldn't go farther. He held back, waiting for her answer. She knew that if she didn't promise him what he wanted, he'd pull away from her, leaving them both miserable. Her heart warmed, realizing he had to care about her — it was more than just sex.

"No regrets," she said at last.

He completed their union with a fast, hard thrust, causing the air to hiss from her lungs. How could she possibly have regrets when she felt so full? She wanted to stay that way forever. She could no longer imagine her life without him. She knew she was in trouble, but as he moved within her body, she didn't care.

He felt so good inside her that she could hardly breathe. He was no longer slow in his movements. He grabbed ahold of her hips so he could thrust in and out of her heat faster and faster. He gripped her firmly in his hands and moved, slapping into her buttocks, shaking her body and making her cry out for more. She tightened around him. An orgasm shook through her once more, almost unending, rippling over her body again and again.

He clutched her hips, his fingers almost bruising in their intensity, as he finally shattered inside her, pumping his seed deep. She felt his release, and it intensified her own pleasure. The moment stretched on for what seemed like hours.

At long last, they both gained control of their breathing. He reluctantly pulled free of her body and moved her to face him.

"I'm sorry, Trinity. That was too rough. I lose control with you too easily." He rubbed his hands down her back. "Are you OK?"

"Mmm" was all she could manage to get out. She was more than OK — she was completely satisfied. She couldn't even keep her eyes open, her body was so sated. She drifted to sleep with his hands still fluttering over her soft curves.

CHAPTER TWENTY-TWO

TRINITY COULDN'T GET comfortable the next day. She was sitting in the den, or one of them, with a movie playing and unable to find a position that didn't make her entire body ache. Her back had been hurting all morning and it seemed to be getting worse. She figured it was just typical pregnancy pain, and she didn't want to alarm Drew, but as the day progressed, the pain progressed, too. Would a hot bath help?

She stood up slowly from the couch, but when she finally made it to her feet, a cramp ripped through her midsection, causing her to double over.

She was so lucky. Drew walked in before she could fall.

He rushed to her side and scooped her into his arms. "What's wrong?"

"I don't know. I'm sure it's nothing." She was barely able to speak, the cramps were gripping her so brutally.

"Something is *obviously* wrong. We're going to the hospital now."

He carried her through the house without even breaking

a sweat. She tried to protest, but he wasn't listening. After situating her carefully in the car and rushing around to his side, he must have broken every speed limit along the way in his haste to get her to the hospital.

He pulled up to the front of the emergency room and rushed her inside. No one stood in his way as he walked her through the throng of people — the intense look on his face probably scared everyone in his path. The doctor he demanded to see had to have been a friend, because the man came running and then rushed her back to a private room, where she found herself hooked up to numerous machines in record time. It gave new meaning to the term *stat*.

As pain continued shooting through her midsection, the doctor explained that she was going into early labor.

It was too soon.

The baby wasn't developed enough.

After looking over her charts and listening to the baby's heartbeat, a worried expression appeared on the doctor's face. But he tried to be positive. "Don't panic. You got here early enough that we should be able to stop the progress of your labor."

Don't panic? *Don't panic?* How could he think she wouldn't panic when he gave her the worst news she could possibly hear?

She looked at Drew. He was trying not to appear worried, but failing miserably. He paced the room as the doctor placed an IV in her arm, and they administered a drug to try to stop the contractions.

"This should stop the labor, but if for some reason your little girl decides to make her entrance into the world early, her chances are good. She's a little over four pounds right now," the doctor tried to reassure them.

"What did I do wrong?" Trinity choked out.

"You've done nothing wrong," the doctor told her. "Our bodies are complex organisms. We don't know why, but sometimes they just don't realize that it's not time for the baby to be born."

Was that reassurance? Whatever.

Trinity lay nearly motionless over the next several hours, not wanting to do anything that could possibly cause the labor to progress. Finally, the drug seemed to work, because the contractions slowed, then stopped. She fell into a fitful sleep as she continued to lie in the hospital bed.

* * *

Drew didn't leave Trinity's side, not for a second. He breathed a sigh of relief when the contractions stopped, but still, he couldn't help but worry. The doctor advised him they could come back at any time. He didn't want the added stress on Trinity, so it was best to let her rest and keep the baby inside as long as possible.

Drew would never be able to forgive himself if something happened to Trinity or his child. He knew he'd been too rough with her the night before when they'd made love. He questioned the doctor, asking whether that could have caused her condition. Though the man insisted that the lovemaking wasn't to blame, Drew didn't believe him. He'd taken her with so much intensity, and surely she was too far along.

Drew continued to pace the room as Trinity came in and out of consciousness. The hospital staff monitored her condition closely, and for now she was stable.

After they made it through the first night without her contractions starting again, Drew started to breathe. The doctor assured them that each day Trinity kept the baby inside her womb gave the fetus a better chance at survival. At this point in the pregnancy, babies grew rapidly.

Once Trinity's stats dropped to a more normal level, the hospital moved her to a private room. Because her cervix was dilated to about four centimeters, the doctor was concerned that labor might have been delayed for only a short period of time, and he wanted her to remain in the hospital, on complete bed rest till the end of her pregnancy. Trinity was willing to agree to anything he asked if it meant better chances for her baby.

"I think we can get you at least one more week along before you go into labor. I doubt that you'll reach full term, but a week can be the difference between the ICU and going home. Your little girl is gaining more weight and getting stronger each day."

She'd been in this freaking hospital room for three days, and Trinity was beyond restless. Couldn't she even take a stupid walk? No one else but her unborn child could make her lie around like this for days on end.

"Why is it we keep meeting in hospital rooms? You know, if you really want to see me that badly, you can just invite me over for dinner." Damien had walked into her room holding a giant vase of flowers, a fistful of balloons, and most importantly, a huge box of chocolates.

"Oh, Damien, you're my hero — that is, *if* you hand over the box of chocolates, immediately."

When he realized that she was speaking through her tears, he stopped teasing her and handed them over. She knew he always got nervous around crying women.

"How are you feeling? Are you going to roast our pretty girl a while longer?" he asked, trying to lighten the mood in the room.

Trinity rubbed her belly. "I'm trying to keep her in as long as possible," she assured him.

"I'm sorry I haven't made it to the new place yet. I had to leave the country for a couple of weeks. This new merger is kicking my butt."

"I've missed you, Damien, especially now, when this disobedient child of mine keeps trying to escape." Once again, her tears were threatening to emerge, and she was having a terrible time fighting them.

"You know I'll never go away, right? I promise that when this deal is over, I'll come over and spend some quality time with you. Heck, I might even change a few diapers."

"I'll hold you to that." She bit into her first chocolate and moaned. When she saw his eyebrows rise, she had to giggle.

Damien stayed with her for the entire afternoon, and she was grateful for the way he kept her mind occupied. Drew even left to give them time together, though she knew he must not have been thrilled to do so. It was just one more thing to add to her ever-growing list of reasons she didn't want to live without Drew.

When Damien finally had to leave, Trinity tried valiantly not to shed tears, but it was useless. She'd miss him. He hugged her several times before he finally managed to pull away.

Drew pulled his chair close to Trinity's bed, grabbed her hand and took a deep breath. She knew he was working up his courage to speak to her about something important, so she waited for him to say what he needed to.

"Trinity, I know you aren't sure about us, but you do know I care about you, right?"

"I think you want to care about me, because you love our daughter."

"I do love our daughter, more than you could ever imagine. I also care about you more than you know. When we're together, everything just feels right. I think over time we can be perfectly happy together. If you give us a real chance, we can be a family."

How could Trinity not be open to hearing what he had to say? She was lying there in the bed and fighting to keep her daughter safe inside her womb. Maybe it was the hormones, the scare of her life, or the man, himself, but she wanted to agree. She wanted her happily-ever-after.

"You're a good man, Drew. I'll admit that."

"Please, Trinity, let me do the right thing for my daughter before she's born. Won't you do me that one thing?"

Trinity didn't understand what he was saying. He'd done all the right things almost from the beginning. What else he could possibly do that he hadn't already? He'd flipped his world upside down to take care of her, bought a new home, took time off from work. She looked at him with her eyes full of question.

And his answer? He reached into his pocket and pulled out a small box. Her eyes widened as she realized what he was talking about. She started shaking her head, but he stopped her.

"Marry me. Take my name and give it to our daughter. Let me be your husband and her father. If you really can't stand it, then you can divorce me, but please don't deliver our daughter without being my wife. I thought we were going to have more time to figure this all out, but she could be born any day, and I need for you to be my wife when she's born"

He spoke with so much conviction that she didn't know how she could deny him.

She had no more arguments — she nodded her head without saying a word.

Drew's face split into a brilliant smile, and he pulled her gently into his arms and hugged her close. "Thank you," he whispered in her ear.

Once she agreed, Drew didn't hesitate. He was on the phone

within minutes, and a few hours later, Derek, Jasmine, and Ryan showed up with a minister in tow. Jasmine handed over a bouquet of flowers, and she placed a tiara on Trinity's head.

Considering that she wasn't allowed to get out of the bed, and that she was wearing a hospital gown — don't look behind! — Trinity felt silly, but she didn't say anything to dampen their enthusiasm.

That Damien wasn't there sent a pang through her, as he was her only family. He was probably going to be very upset with her when he found out that she got married. Of course, he'd say she didn't need to rush – that's what best friends were for – to save you from yourself.

"We'll do this again the right way later, but for now, it's the best we can do on such short notice," Jasmine told her.

"Thank you, Jasmine. You really didn't have to do anything at all," Trinity said. She knew she must look a wreck, but she wasn't even allowed up for a shower, only sponge baths. She didn't exactly feel like a blushing bride. And because it hurt her heart a little to think about it, she pushed the thought from her mind.

Fifteen minutes and she was married. A ceremony without much ceremony.

Ryan left the room and came back with a beautiful cake and sparkling cider. She got choked up as Drew fed her a piece of the cake, then leaned down and kissed her lips. He seemed so happy, so she must have made the right choice.

Ryan held up his glass in a toast. "I know this isn't a traditional wedding by any means, but none of that matters. What matters is that the two of you love each other, and are going to have a beautiful baby girl soon. There will be plenty of time later to do everything the right way. May you have many romantic days, and far more passionate nights."

Trinity could feel a blush staining her cheeks at his words. It might not have been her dream wedding, but it was perfect nonetheless.

Oh, no. As she looked at Drew, she realized that she was head over heels, completely and totally in love with the man. How on earth had that happened? She had no idea at what point she'd let down the walls, but she knew the door was open, and if he decided to leave, she'd never pick up all the pieces of her shattered heart.

She couldn't say it was at any one particular moment that she fell in love with him. It was more like several smaller moments over the last several months. Drew was simply too hard to resist.

She'd feel more confident if she knew how he really felt. She knew he loved their daughter, and she knew he cared about her. But was it enough? Only time would tell.

CHAPTER TWENTY-THREE

BARELY THIRTY-SIX WEEKS into her pregnancy, Trinity's contractions came back, and nothing the doctor did could stop them. She prayed she'd kept her child inside long enough.

Once her water broke, she knew the delivery was coming. She'd hoped to stretch it for even a day or two more. The pain wouldn't have mattered to her — she'd have endured anything to give her baby girl more time inside her womb, safe and sound.

"Trinity, your labor is moving along rapidly," the doctor said. "We need to move you to the birthing room. It looks like your daughter is anxious to meet her parents."

An aide wheeled Trinity down the hallway with Drew at her side. The touch of his hand against hers, grounded her — it somehow let her know everything would be fine.

And the doctor agreed. "Everything looks good, Trinity. Her heartbeat is strong, and she's put on good weight this last week and a half. I know that doesn't seem like much time, but for a baby, it can make all the difference between life and death."

"You'll both be OK, baby. I know it. Just hang on a little

while longer. Just think, soon, we'll be holding our daughter."

All her fears still came rushing back. "It's too soon," she whispered. She was afraid to speak too loudly. She didn't want to put any negative thoughts in the air, but she had to say something. The terror was suffocating her.

"You've done everything you were supposed to do. I know she'll be strong, just like her mother," Drew told her, then bent down to kiss her gently.

She took a long breath and got ready to push.

A nurse placed her legs in stirrups and checked her dilation.

"You're ready," the doctor said, "so the next time you feel a contraction, I want you to use all your strength and push."

She didn't have to wait long before the pain came ripping through her. She'd never felt anything like it. The sublime beauty of childbirth, eh? Not quite. It was as if her guts were turning inside out and she were going to explode. Sweat broke out on her brow and she screamed as she pushed down with all her might.

"That's really good, Trinity. I can see her head. I think she's going to come out with only a few pushes. I know it's hard, but you need to relax for a moment, and then push just like that when you get your next contraction."

The next one hit before she was ready, but she did what the doctor said, gripping Drew's hand tightly in hers.

"Very good; she's crowning. We need to get her head out, so as soon as it hits, give it all you've got."

She wanted to bash the guy's head in. It was so easy for him to tell her to give it all she had. He wasn't the one trying to pass something the size of a watermelon out of a small opening in his body.

Right after Drew rubbed a cloth over her sweating brow, the next contraction hit with the force of a tornado. She didn't see how she wasn't ripped in half from the horrible pain.

She screamed again. She was pushing as hard as she could and felt a burning pain as the baby's head came out. The doctor was doing something —what was it? Did she even want to know? And then the next contraction hit even harder and she pushed again without any words from anyone, and she felt more burning. She could see it now. She would probably die right there on the table, before she even saw her daughter.

The contractions were right on top of each other, and she barely had time to catch her breath before the intense urge to push again hit her. Two more times, and then relief. Her daughter had finally emerged.

She looked up to see the doctor stick something into the baby's mouth, and then the most amazing sound surrounded Trinity, the angry wail of her daughter's intense displeasure at being taken from her warm home of eight months.

The nurse quickly wrapped the child in a blanket and laid her on Trinity's chest, and the new mother was finally looking into the squinting eyes of her baby girl. She was the most beautiful thing she'd ever seen. Trinity could see that her daughter was trying to open her eyes, but the bright lights must have made it a difficult task. Her baby was crying in an achingly pathetic voice, and Trinity sobbed along with her.

The girl was so tiny that Trinity didn't see how it was possible that she could be OK, but the newborn looked pink and beautiful beneath the slimy paste on her body. Trinity looked at Drew and was amazed to see a tear slide down his cheek as he touched his daughter for the first time. Her heart swelled even more.

"We need to take her over here and make sure she's doing well," the nurse told her in a kindly voice. "We'll bring her back right away if all her vitals check out."

The woman picked the baby up, and Trinity's tears were now falling at the empty feeling of not having her daughter in her arms.

Drew once again bent to kiss his wife. "She looks healthy and strong, Trinity. You did a very good job."

"I hope so." She didn't take her eyes off her daughter, who was lying helplessly under the warming lights. At least the nurses didn't seem to be in a panic as they checked the child's vitals.

The doctor gave Trinity a shot that numbed her. Although she knew she had to look pretty darn frightening, Drew was staring at her as if she were the most beautiful thing he'd ever seen. Her heart was filled with warmth, which she needed, since she couldn't seem to stop shaking now that the birthing was over.

The nurses cleaned her and lifted her onto a new bed, causing more pain for a few minutes. But the heated blankets now under and on top of her made the pain worth it, because she was finally starting to warm up.

"It looks as if you kept her safe inside for a long enough time," the doctor finally said, "because she's healthy. Her lungs are fully developed and she won't need oxygen. She's a little underweight at only four pounds eight ounces, so we'll want to keep her here until she's over five pounds. But other than that, you have a healthy, beautiful baby girl"

His words filled Trinity with relief. Their baby was going to be fine. Trinity would have stayed in bed for the next month straight if she could have given the baby more time, but she was still going to be OK.

"Can I hold her again?" Trinity asked.

"Of course you can," the nurse said, and she brought the baby over and placed her back in Trinity's arms. She was now wrapped in a warm blanket, and mother and daughter watched each other in fascination.

"How are you doing, princess?" Trinity asked as she rubbed the child's head.

Her daughter looked at her with those beautiful blue eyes all newborns have. She blinked a few times, and Trinity couldn't believe she was actually holding her in her arms.

"Do you want to hold your daughter?" she asked Drew.

"I'm afraid I'll break her. I've never held such a tiny baby."

"You'll be perfect at it," Trinity told him.

He leaned down and gently picked the infant up and cradled her to his chest. The look of complete and overwhelming love on his face made more tears fall down Trinity's cheeks. The man obviously adored his daughter, and she knew she'd done the right thing in marrying him. Even if he never loved her, he'd always love his little girl, and that meant more than anything else.

* * *

"She weighs nothing — it's like I'm holding only a blanket," Drew said in awe as he held the child close.

He couldn't believe how amazing his baby girl was. She was tiny but so perfectly formed. He had never in his life loved anything as he loved his daughter. It was overwhelming in its intensity. He loved his family and he loved Trinity, although that was hard for him to accept, but the love for his daughter was unlike anything he'd ever experienced.

As he held her and looked down at his wife, everything was perfect. He knew he couldn't live without either of them. He'd fight to the death, dammit, to keep their family intact. He could now understand what his cousin Derek had gone through, and he felt a bit of guilt at how much he'd teased the poor man.

Drew had all the money in the world, but he'd never felt truly rich until this moment, with his newborn daughter held tightly against him and his wife looking up with love in her beautiful eyes.

"It's time to move you back to your own room," the nurse said.

Drew laid the baby back in Trinity's arms for the trip. She looked relieved to have her child back, and she didn't take her eyes off the baby the entire way. He doubted that she'd have noticed if the building were falling down around them, she was so fascinated by their daughter.

When they'd arrived in the room, the nurse helped Trinity sit up in bed, then brought a tray of food. Drew took the baby again and sat in the chair next to her bed so she could eat.

"Are you nursing, or should I make up a bottle?" the nurse asked.

"I'm nursing."

"After you're done with your meal, we should try and get her to eat. She won't be very interested at first, but she'll soon gain an appetite."

"OK."

Drew stepped out of the room, to give her privacy and to let his family know that his daughter was born. They were all in the waiting room, most likely pacing in true Titan fashion.

"It's a girl."

Drew's words were greeted by silence for about two seconds before everyone began talking at once.

"When did she arrive?"

"What's taken so long?"

"Don't you think you could have come out sooner?"

"We've been so worried!"

"Sorry, I know I took too long, but I was so anxious about everything, I didn't want to leave Trinity for even a few minutes. She's doing great, though, and our daughter is a beautiful pink color. She's under five pounds, so they'll keep her here a few days to make sure she puts on a little more weight, but other than that, everything's fine."

"I guess we'll forgive you," Jasmine said. "That is, we'll forgive you if you take me in to see my niece." The look in her eye told him that he was a ways off from being forgiven.

"We need to give her a few more minutes. She's nursing right now. The first few times can be difficult, I guess."

"Well, yeah. Try having your nipples sucked on all day and night, and see how you feel," Jasmine said with a roll of her eyes.

"Why don't we test that out," Derek said with a leer at his wife.

"Behave," Jasmine told him, but she was smiling. From the look on her face, it seemed she'd be willing to take him up on his offer.

Drew held them back as long as he could, but they threatened to trample him if he didn't let them in to see the mother and child. Luckily, they arrived after she finished nursing. None of the family could get enough of how tiny and beautiful the baby was.

"Oh, my gosh, she makes Britney seem so big now," Jasmine said as she cuddled the baby close. "I want to have ten more of these, Derek."

"You can have as many as you want. We can get started tonight, in fact."

Jasmine giggled and passed the baby to Ryan. He cradled her gently with a look of awe.

"She's just so tiny," he whispered. She looked even smaller against him — one of his hands was the length of her body. "I'm afraid I'll break her." He looked at Drew with panic in his eyes.

"Don't look at me. I'm afraid I'll break her, too."

"You guys wouldn't do anything that would harm her, not in a million years," Trinity told the men. They soon handed the baby back to Trinity, and she took her greedily in her arms.

"What's her name?" Derek asked.

Trinity and Drew looked at each other. They hadn't really discussed names, and in all the excitement since the birth, neither of them had thought about it. Drew had no idea whether she'd picked anything out.

"I have a favorite aunt named Cindi," Drew said. "I've always liked that name."

"OK, then. Her name is Cindi."

"Hello there, Cindi Titan," Ryan said. "Welcome to the family." He brushed his hand against her soft head.

Drew liked the sound of that. His beautiful baby girl, Cindi Titan, had arrived safe, sound and healthy.

When Trinity started yawning, the family said their goodbyes. Drew carefully picked Cindi up and laid her in the bassinet next to her bed. If the baby made a peep, Trinity would wake up and be able to tend to her. Exhausted from all her labors, the mother fell asleep before the last Titan left the room.

* * *

Drew worked his typical magic. The baby was kept in the hospital for four days while she put on weight, and he made sure that he and Trinity were with her the whole time. Normally, the mother was released after two days if she was healthy and ready —and she was. But she couldn't leave her newborn there. Drew made sure she stayed as a patient so she could still have a comfortable bed and a private room. That he was a billionaire didn't hurt.

Trinity didn't care how he'd done it. She only cared that she could keep Cindi with her, because she wasn't willing to spend even a minute away from her daughter, let alone an entire night. When the doctor finally gave them the OK to bring Cindi home, Trinity was more than ready to get out of the hospital. She wanted her own bed, and she really wanted her daily routine to resume. It would be better now that she wasn't sporting an extra thirty pounds of baby on the inside.

CHAPTER TWENTY-FOUR

A MONTH OLD? Already? Trinity looked at her daughter and smiled. The time was flying by too quickly, and she wanted nothing more than to stop the clock.

She and Drew had come to a truce of sorts. They were both mesmerized with their little girl, and he'd stayed home nonstop for two weeks after she'd come home from the hospital, but one of his resorts was having difficulties, and he'd left two weeks ago. She missed him terribly, and that surprised her.

He set up a video-conferencing system because he couldn't bear to not see his daughter every single day. He'd even had a private camera hung over her crib so he could click his computer on and watch his little girl sleep. Trinity found his love overwhelming.

Of course, as she looked down at the child, it was impossible to imagine anyone not loving that little girl like crazy.

Trinity was also grateful to have Jasmine around, especially because Drew was gone for such a long period of time. The home was so large, and she couldn't help but be lonely. Jasmine came over often to keep her company, telling Jasmine that she got lonely herself, with Derek working, and Jacob at school.

Both women were excited in the extreme about their business venture. Today was their last day of getting the final touches done, and their grand opening was coming tomorrow. They'd hired a few employees, and Jasmine had a nanny who'd be at the shop to help with the two babies. It all seemed too unreal to be true.

Trinity had been too worn out from the hard pregnancy and delivery to be the one to close her old shop down, and it had been bittersweet to enter the empty shop after it had been cleared out.

She was moving on to a better place, so it wasn't as if it were the end. But she had to mourn At least she'd had Jasmine's support when she did the final walk-through.

Drew had hired staff for the house, so she was never truly alone, but it wasn't the same thing as having either her husband there or her best friend. But she was getting pretty close to Maria, their cook. Maria was close to the age her mom would have been, and she was full of life and laughter. The woman was a phenomenal cook as well. Even Jasmine — most definitely a critic — liked Maria's food.

Trinity heard Jasmine's laughter about two seconds before her friend entered the room.

"I love that little dress," Jasmine said. "She looks so adorable today. I can't believe how much she keeps growing." She pulled Cindi into her arms, and the baby cooed at her. Jasmine laughed even more.

"It's really amazing how quickly they grow," Trinity said. "Where's Britney?"

"I left her at home with the nanny. We're going to be putting the final merchandise out and I thought it would be easier. She's walking all over, now."

"I love that Cindi is gaining weight, but I'm grateful she can't get away yet. It would be much harder to keep an eye on her while we're down there."

"Ryan got the cribs and swings set up for us," Jasmine said. "I think the girls are going to do great, but our first few days are going to be hectic, so I'll leave Britney at home, although it will kill me a little. If she was still nursing, I couldn't do that."

"Yes, nursing can definitely be a blessing and a curse," Trinity said.

She was the food source for her daughter, and the child, because she was still so tiny, ate far more often.

"Oh, Trinity, I'm desperately trying to fight the baby blues right now. Britney is almost a year old, and holding Cindi all the time is making my womb jump. Of course, Derek is ready anytime I want to have another one, but I want to wait at least six more months before we start trying. Of course, I never get tired of practicing." Jasmine was sporting a satisfied grin.

How could Trinity not be jealous of her friend? Drew hadn't touched her since the week before the baby was born. He'd blamed himself for sending her into early labor —ridiculous! That was probably just an excuse. She still had baby weight to take off, and she was always so worn out that she was sure she wasn't looking her best. The man wasn't even kissing her, and why should he? She looked a wreck all the time. It would be so nice if he felt about her the same way Derek felt about Jasmine.

No, no, no. She had to push those thoughts aside because they just didn't do her any good. The important thing was that they were making their marriage work. Their daughter could have security and love, which was far more important than her own needs.

"Are you ready to leave?" Jasmine asked her.

"Yes, we need to before I lose all energy. I'm afraid I'm going to spend too much time in that break room Ryan built us."

"I couldn't believe how amazing the room was — he really thought of everything. He's an absolute genius at design."

They climbed into Jasmine's car and drove the short distance to their shop. The way Ryan had done everything they'd asked, and more, still inspired awe in Trinity. Everything was beautiful, inside and out. As they stepped from the vehicle, they spotted Ryan doing some final touch-up paint.

"You're here late," he said as he opened the back door of the car and pulled out Cindi's seat. Trinity was thankful that her daughter was fast asleep; it meant that she could work for a little while.

"It's hard to get out the door when you're dealing with babies," Jasmine said. "They need to be changed and fed, and then when you think you're ready to go, they spit up on you, and you have to start all over again." The woman was all talk, though. It was obvious she loved being a mother.

"It can't be all that hard — not that I'd know anything about it," Ryan remarked. His words may have said he was relieved he didn't, but he seemed more than ready for his own.

"Yes, Ryan. You're a confirmed bachelor, for sure," Jasmine said with a twinkle in her eyes.

"Do you want me to put Cindi into the crib?" Ryan asked.

"No, she's comfortable in her seat. Just undo the latches and tuck her blanket around her. I just changed and fed her, so she should sleep for a couple hours."

He seemed disappointed, but he did what she asked without complaint. Still, she'd have to keep an eye on him, just to make sure he didn't wake Cindi on purpose so he could carry her around. It seemed all the Titan men tended to do that.

"Don't you dare wake her, Ryan."

"I won't," he said with a grumble that sounded an awful lot like "*women*."

Trinity fought back the laughter.

She glanced around the showroom, which was ready to be set up. The space was huge, with custom-built display shelves. The coolers for her flowers were framed in wood, and splashes of color drew the eye to strategic points.

She walked behind the counters then sat down behind one of them and spun her chair. She couldn't wait to set up at her workstation. It had everything she'd ever wanted, and more. If she got tired, the break room was only a few feet behind her work space, and inside sat a soft sofa that she had a feeling she'd take many naps on.

Trinity walked reluctantly from her area over to Jasmine's side of the shop. Jasmine was in heaven in the huge cooking area, and the counter was almost a replica of Trinity's. It was just longer, and it had attached stools.

Jasmine already had several glass cases set out, just waiting for her goodies to fill them. The kitchen had top-of-the-line appliances and plenty of room for people to move around. She had a limited menu, and was only serving breakfast and lunch, but Trinity had a feeling she was going to be busy, day and night, because her food was excellent.

"What are you working on?" Trinity asked her.

"I'm getting the soup of the day ready for tomorrow. This one is better if it has a night to sit in the fridge and develop its flavor before it's cooked."

A couple of people were busy working on dishes for the next day, but Jasmine was a major fan of freshness, and some things had to wait until the next morning.

The smell of bread rising made Trinity's stomach growl.

"I've got to get out of here and set up fans to blow the smell away from me, because I'll never lose this weight with you cooking all these delights." Trinity practically ran from the kitchen. Jasmine's laughter followed her across the shop.

Trinity soon got busy setting out the last of her gift items on the pristine shelves, and with the help of her two employees, she began making several bouquets. She wanted the cases full of everything imaginable, from single rose vases to huge baskets. If she sold even half the display, she'd be ecstatic.

She was just finishing a basket when the monitor signaled that Cindi was awake. She went to get her, but Ryan beat her to it. He was pulling her out of the seat and talking baby talk. Cindi blew bubbles at him as she stared at her uncle with her big blue eyes. He carried her around for a while, until she decided it was time to eat, then he reluctantly handed her over.

Trinity was more than happy to take her back to the break room and have time alone with her daughter. She sat in the rocking chair and enjoyed the sounds of Cindi's hungry slurps as her child gulped down her milk as if it were the last meal she'd get.

Her daughter had liked eating from day one. Trinity rubbed the baby's head and sang to her softly.

Trinity felt her eyes getting heavy as she finished feeding Cindi, and raised her to her shoulder for burping. She couldn't wait until she was back to having all her energy again. Hell, since giving birth, she hadn't made it through one day without a nap.

Once Trinity and Jasmine were satisfied that the shop was ready for opening the next day, they called it a night. They couldn't deny their sense of pride as they looked around at what they'd helped to create. Opening day should be a complete success.

As Trinity laid Cindi down for the night and slipped into her huge bed all alone, she found herself fighting back tears. She'd really wanted Drew to be with her for the grand opening. She knew her small business was nothing compared to the billion-dollar resorts he owned, but it was special to her — a huge accomplishment. OK. His absence was unavoidable, but she had to feel disappointment. She wondered whether he would have made being there a priority if their relationship were stronger.

Those questions weren't going to get answers that night, so she closed her eyes and finally drifted to sleep with tears drying on her face.

CHAPTER TWENTY-FIVE

YOU'VE DONE AN excellent job solving this problem. Anything you need over the next month will have to go through the home office. As of right now, I'm on vacation, and there aren't any exceptions for me coming off it."

After Drew spoke to the circle of men around the table, he thrust his papers into his briefcase. He was in a hurry to leave.

He'd been stuck on the small island off the coast of Spain for two weeks. If he didn't want to miss the grand opening of his wife's new business, he had to get his jet into the air within the hour. She hadn't pleaded for him to come home, but he knew his presence would mean a lot to her. He didn't care if it cost him the deal. He was leaving, one way or the other.

He shook hands with the men and quickly left. His driver was waiting, and the jet ready. They made it to the airport in record time.

He could barely contain his excitement as he boarded. He'd never felt such urgency to return home before. He'd missed his baby girl with an incredible ache. He'd also missed his wife. He needed to tell her how important she was to him, and he needed her to accept the fact that they were going to stay together forever. If the last two weeks were any indication, he knew he couldn't live his life without Trinity and his daughter.

It wasn't just a matter of needing to be with them; it was the fact that he just wasn't complete without them. No business deal he could make anywhere in the world, no matter what a coup it was, could bring him as much joy as he felt lying next to Trinity, or rocking his daughter to sleep. He'd found his place in life, the true center of his existence, and he needed to get back to it.

As Drew waited for cruising altitude, he didn't think he'd be able to sleep, but before he knew it, the captain was speaking over the intercom, telling him to prepare for landing. Drew looked out the window as the sun rose in the sky and his anticipation rose to a fever pitch. He could hardly wait to pull both Trinity and Cindi into his arms. It was good to be home — now he just had to get to the new shop before it opened.

A driver was waiting for him at the airport, and he was *finally* on his way to the shop. He had an hour's drive, and only forty minutes to get there.

"There will be a five-hundred-dollar bonus if you get me to my destination in thirty minutes or less," Drew said.

The man hit the gas, and Drew smiled. Money always spoke volumes.

As they pulled into the parking lot after exactly twenty-six minutes, Drew was a little thankful, they'd made it in one piece. He slipped the driver his promised bonus, then slipped around back and let himself into the employee entrance. He immediately searched for his wife and spotted her at the counter. Damn, he'd missed her.

"Mmm, you smell like heaven. Want to sneak into the back with me?" Drew wrapped his arms around Trinity, and her startled expression turned into a beaming smile.

"I didn't think you'd be here."

"I wasn't going to miss this — not for anything. You really do smell good. That offer's still on the table if you want to go in the back. As a matter of fact, any table will do for what I have in mind. On it, under it, against it…"

"Drew, I can't leave, but I'll take you up on that later."

Drew drank her in for a few moments before he bent his head down to take her lips. In a matter of seconds, his body was hurting, he was so hungry for her. It was probably too soon for them to make love, but he could think of other ways of pleasing her — and himself.

"I missed you and Cindi. I finally hired a new executive so I won't have to travel nearly as often, but when I do, I'm taking you both with me, because I can't bear to be apart from you both."

"I missed you, too, Drew." Admitting that made her feel shy, but she couldn't help herself.

"I'm taking you out for a special celebratory dinner tonight," he said, and he kissed her again. When he finally lifted his head, he felt almost light-headed. She was stunning with her flushed cheeks and hooded eyes. He was sorely tempted to demand they put the grand opening off for an hour…or three.

"That sounds perfect," she finally replied, breaking the spell he was under.

That was a good thing. They could have been very embarrassed when one of the employees came to let them know the doors would be opening in one minute. Drew reluctantly let Trinity go and went to find his daughter.

Cindi was just starting to stir in her crib, and as he bent down to pull her into his arms, her eyes opened, causing a slight tickle in his throat. She was still tiny, but so beautiful and healthy, and he'd missed the subtle scent only she had.

He walked back into the main part of the store and found his cousins. The three men watched as a rush of people came flooding through the doors. They were filled with pride for Jasmine and Trinity, who'd worked so hard for something they were passionate about. The women were beaming as they rang up sale after sale.

* * *

Trinity kept looking up, overwhelmed at the sight of her handsome husband, who was holding Cindi gently in his arms. She was busy for the next several hours, but found that she wanted nothing more than to break away, and hold her daughter while Drew held them both. She'd always wanted the shop, and she was proud it was having such a successful opening day, but she finally realized that being with her husband and daughter outweighed her need for success.

She had a competent staff and would be more than happy to be there part time. Jasmine told her that she'd be working minimal hours herself, as she couldn't bear to be away from her family for long.

Trinity realized there was nothing wrong with depending on Drew. Even if the man never loved her the way she loved him, she'd be happy to just be a family — as long as they were together.

Damien walked up and kissed her on the cheek. "I'd like to order every bouquet in the shop," he told her.

"You said you wouldn't be able to make it today." A huge grin split Trinity's face. Her day was officially perfect now that all the people she loved were in the same room.

"I threw business out the window. Today is about my best

friend and beautiful niece."

Trinity threw her arms around him and held on tight.

"I think there are holes being burned into my back," Damien said with a laugh.

When he dipped her low and whipped her back up, she had to giggle. She looked over at Drew, who looked as if he was grumbling something to his cousins. She liked the thought he might be a bit jealous.

A customer came up. "Excuse me, Miss. Can you help me?"

"I'm sorry, Damien, but it looks like I'm being summoned," she said, trying to hide her reluctance.

She gave him another hug before she got back to work. He walked over to where the Titan men were standing, and she caught a glimpse of Drew slugging him in the arm. *Ouch*, she thought, but Damien laughed, and the men continued to talk for a while, so it must not have been that bad. She sighed when Damien slipped out the doors.

She broke away a few times to feed her daughter, but other than that, she was swamped all day. By the time they were able to leave, she was pretty dead on her feet. Drew took her home, instead of out on the town, then massaged her feet while she fed Cindi. She lay back and enjoyed the feel of his hands on her.

After they put the baby to bed, Drew led her to their bedroom. He pushed her gently and sweetly onto the bed. It almost killed her that her body wasn't ready yet for lovemaking. And she had further anxieties. She still wasn't back to prepregnancy weight, and that made her nervous about him touching her at all. As he began rubbing her back and sides, she pulled away.

"I want to touch you. I know you aren't ready, but that doesn't mean I can't kiss you and enjoy your curves," he said, and he kissed her breath away.

She could feel her cheeks heat. "I still have this extra weight from the baby."

"You're stunning, Trinity. Your body is perfect. Don't ever try to hide from me, because I love every inch of you."

As if to prove his point, he took her hand and pressed it against his rock-solid arousal. She practically drooled.

"But...but... You haven't touched me since the baby was born, and I thought you were repulsed by me."

"How could you ever believe I'd think something like that? I could *never* be turned off by you. I was just feeling so much guilt about our lovemaking the night before you went into the hospital. You make me go crazy, and I was so rough with you, and I haven't trusted myself to be with you until now."

"Drew, you'd never hurt me. You please me in ways I never knew were possible before I met you. You've given me so much, and I can't imagine my life without you. I know I've been stubborn, and a bit of a pain, but I love you, and I want our marriage to be the real thing."

"Oh, Trinity, I've loved you for so long. Before you came along, I'd never realized how empty my life was. I missed you the moment you left our private paradise, and I was overjoyed to find you pregnant with my child. I know I've made a lot of mistakes along the way, but loving you has been the best thing I've ever done."

Drew pulled her close so he could devour her mouth. Neither of them could breathe by the time he pulled back. He began exploring her throat, then moved down the slopes of her breasts. Her body ached as she cried out in frustration that they couldn't be joined together.

She might not be able to make love with Drew right then, but she could certainly make sure he was satisfied. She pushed him over and slowly unbuttoned his shirt, and then ran her tongue over his muscled chest.

A slight sheen of sweat was breaking out on his tanned skin.

"Baby, I can't take much more," he said through gritted teeth as he tried pulling her back up.

She shook his hands off. She reached his lower stomach and gently nipped the taut skin.

"You don't have to do this," he growled, empowering her to want to do more — so much more.

She said nothing as she slowly unbuttoned his pants and pulled them and his boxer shorts off. His magnificent length sprang out, showing her how very turned on he was.

She kissed her way back up his legs and smiled when his body quivered. His breathing was heavy and his head was thrown back as he groaned in pleasure. She reached the top of his thighs and his body lifted off the bed as her hand rubbed across the head of his arousal.

She slipped her tongue out and licked the bead of moisture off his tip, making him cry out. She'd never before felt so sexy or powerful in bed. It was a euphoric feeling, and she wouldn't have ever done this for another man. She'd been much slower than her friends in exploring her sexuality. She was glad she'd waited — glad it was for him, and only him. She wrapped her fingers around his satin-covered shaft, loving how hard he was. She moved her hand up and down while gripping him tightly. Then she lowered her head and took him into her mouth.

As her tongue flicked over his shaft and her hand continued to work its magic, he groaned - encouraging her to keep going. She tightened her mouth around him and began sucking him deeper inside her mouth. He grabbed her head, holding her tightly against him, as she continued to pleasure him. How she loved the feel of his fingers clutching her hair!

His body began to tense and he pulled her head back —

though she protested, wanting more of his taste.

"I'm not going to last," he croaked out.

Nice. She smiled and ran her tongue across his head. And she continued to stroke him with her hand. Faster. He finally cried out as his release shot from him.

She stared in fascination as his engorged staff pumped in her hand. It was the sexiest thing she'd ever watched in her life. His body shuddered in pleasure as she used his own release to slide her hand up and down his still-quivering manhood. She continued to rub him until every last ounce of his seed spilled out. And then she couldn't resist flicking her tongue one last time over his beautiful shaft. He convulsed at her gentle touch and she had to gloat. His response to her showed her pure feminine power.

She slowly kissed her way back up his abs and chest until she finally brought their lips together. His kiss was gentle as he rubbed his tongue against her bottom lip. He brought his hand to the outside of her silk panties and rubbed.

Trinity was now the one writhing in pleasure, her body on fire already from watching his pleasure.

"I can't..." she started to say, but as he slipped the panties away and touched her swollen bud, her protest stopped with a gasp of pleasure.

"I won't go inside, but I need to touch you," he said into her mouth. She moaned her acceptance.

He continued kissing her, and he flicked his fingers over the center of her desire. She wanted so much more. She wanted him connecting their bodies together, and it nearly destroyed her that her body wasn't ready. Not yet. But her stomach quivered with pure pleasure at what he was doing with his hand.

She jerked in surprise as an intense orgasm washed through her. He continued to stroke her, and wave after wave of pleasure washed through her. She finally collapsed against his chest.

Drew pulled her close and drew the coverlet over them while her head lay against his chest. She fell asleep to the sound of his beating heart, knowing that nothing could be as wonderful as this moment.

CHAPTER TWENTY-SIX

HER DAUGHTER WAS about to be a year old. Time had slipped by, and Trinity felt happy and secure. Drew had a surprise of some sort planned for her, and she was almost giddy trying to imagine what it might be.

He'd already given her everything she could ever want, and so much more. She had a surprise for him, too. She rubbed her belly in anticipation. She'd just found out she was pregnant again. She knew it was too soon, as Cindi was only a year old, and she'd hoped to wait for another year, but though it would be hard, she had to be excited. Drew loved Cindi so much that he'd been willing to have their next child when she was only a couple of months old. He and his cousins couldn't get enough of the kids — particularly Ryan, lately.

She'd noticed a change in Ryan and she was worried about him. He'd seemed stressed out, and she wondered if maybe a woman was causing those circles under his eyes. She and Jasmine were determined to find out what was going on.

He'd recently purchased a home near them, and they were both thinking that he was getting ready to settle down. They'd get information out of him sooner or later. Jasmine was sporting a gigantic grin when she walked into the room and interrupted Trinity's thoughts.

"Are you ready to go?"

"You have to tell me what's going on, Jasmine," Trinity said. "It's an honor thing among women."

Jasmine had been as secretive as Drew, and they were driving Trinity crazy.

"I'm sorry, but I can't give it away. Let me tell you, though, I'm a bit jealous. You have a man who loves you very much. If I didn't have my own amazing husband, I wouldn't be nearly as happy for you."

"I just want to let you know that the next time you're overcome with anxiety, I'm going to sit back and smile."

Trinity followed Jasmine from the house. She still had no clue where they were going, or what was happening.

They drove out of town and pulled up to a recreation hall, and then walked inside. She looked around in confusion.

Jasmine was beaming.

"What is all this?" Trinity gasped.

"Drew promised to give you a real wedding, so he planned it all. I couldn't believe you didn't get suspicious when I was questioning you about your perfect dress, or what kind of place you'd like. And then the fitting of the supposed ball dress was priceless. Has anyone ever told you that you're incredibly gullible?"

"I had no idea."

The room was filled with people, and Trinity just stared. She was rushed to a makeup area, and a couple of people started playing with her hair, while two others started working on her fingernails and toenails. Within two hours, Trinity was transformed. When she was finally allowed to look in the mirror, she saw diamonds dripping from her hair. If they were real, she'd probably freak out, so she decided not to think about it.

Jasmine slipped behind her and placed the same tiara on her head that that Trinity had worn in the hospital on her head. That one piece from her first wedding completed her look and also completed her joy.

They walked into a dressing room and Trinity felt tears fall as she looked at the delicate gown hanging against the wall. It was perfect in every single way. Jasmine and Drew had done an amazing job to make sure her dress was everything she could ever want.

Jasmine helped Trinity put on the gown, and as the layers of silk floated over her body and Jasmine tightened it up, Trinity truly felt like a princess. She stepped into the exquisite heels and looked in the mirror again, barely able to recognize herself in the reflection.

Jasmine donned her own stunning gown, and Trinity could hardly wait to get to Drew. She knew he'd look incredibly handsome. When the women stepped outside, the beautiful convertible Jaguar with bows on it was a particular treat. The driver was wearing a tuxedo and top hat. Trinity giggled at the romance of it all.

They were assisted into the vehicle, and the driver made his way slowly down the road. It didn't take long before they pulled up to a secluded church. It looked out of place in the middle of the woods, and Trinity wondered how he'd found the place.

"I hope you don't mind, but this is where I had my wedding. Derek had it fixed up for me, and I thought you'd love it, as well," Jasmine said.

"It's perfect, Jasmine, and exactly what I would have chosen," she said, trying hard not to let her tears start flowing again.

The driver stepped around and helped them from the vehicle. Trinity looked around at the decorations, done so perfectly. A narrow red carpet led up the path and over the steps. Each step boasted a huge floral arrangement, and bows ran along the banisters. Everything was done perfectly, and with real thought put into it.

When the door opened and Damien walked out, devastating in his tux and top hat, Trinity lost control of her battle with her tears. How was this man still single? He was a catch by anyone's standards. OK, just a friend by hers.

"Hello, beautiful. May I please escort you into the church?"

"You're going to ruin my makeup," Trinity replied with a hiccup.

Damien wrapped his arms around her and held her close for several moments, allowing her to pull herself together. Finally, she stopped sniffling and he moved back and took her chin in his hand.

"You're stunning, wonderful, and I kick myself that I didn't chase after you. Now, let's get you inside before Drew comes out here, attempts to kick my butt, and I have to embarrass him in front of his bride."

Trinity started laughing. She knew he was kidding. They were friends and and never would have been more. She knew she never would've married him — she loved him too much to do that to him.

She nodded her head, unable to speak, and placed her arm through his.

The music started and they made their way forward. Trinity took a deep breath —one step at a time, she told herself. She looked only to the front as they entered the church, and then all thoughts evaporated as Drew came into sight.

He was a vision in his tuxedo. He was standing with his

father and cousin next to him, with Jasmine and Derek on the other side, and the family made such a beautiful sight that she felt like she couldn't even breathe. This was forever.

Their eyes were locked as she made her way toward him. When Damien placed her hand in Drew's, she could swear electricity flowed between her and the man she'd married once and was marrying again. The minister said the usual words, and she repeated the vows where she was supposed to, but she had no idea how she managed, because she was almost faint with happiness.

Soon, the minister pronounced them remarried, and Drew pulled her into his arms. He kissed her with so much passion and longing that it felt as if they really were marrying for the first time. Derek cleared his throat, and Drew slowly drew away. She blushed as the crowd broke into applause.

Drew slipped her arm through his and walked her up the aisle. He almost dragged her out the door and took her around the back of the church where he had huge tents set up, and music playing. He directed her straight to the dance floor and molded her body to his.

"You're stunning," he whispered in her ear, causing a shiver of desire to run down her spine. She loved him and couldn't believe she'd ever fought being with him. He brought his lips to hers, and her stomach quivered with desire. She didn't know how many songs they danced through, but eventually she noticed other couples had joined them on the dance floor.

Trinity looked at Jasmine, who was wrapped tightly in Derek's arms. The two of them acted like newlyweds themselves, as he spun her around. Something he said made her giggle in delight, and then she blushed red and looked around in shame.

"It's time to cut the cake," someone called out, and Drew led her to a table with a huge four-tiered cake. He cut a piece off and fed it to her oh, so sweetly — even though the crowd was insisting that they get a little messier. He ate the small piece of cake she was holding, then sucked her finger into his mouth to lick away the frosting.

She felt the pull of his lips deep inside her stomach, and a shiver of desire raced through her. She watched Drew's eyes narrow in passion, and she wanted nothing more than to get into a room with him. She didn't even care where it was, but she wanted her husband — now. In the heat of the moment, he started to drag her of, but Ryan grabbed his arm.

"Not so fast there, Romeo. It's time for your toasts."

Drew groaned, but Ryan just laughed as he took Trinity's arm. She looked back longingly at her husband.

After Jasmine appeared to lead her off to change, Trinity had to blurt out her news.

"I'm pregnant."

Jasmine squeaked with delight and threw her arms around Trinity.

"Oh, my gosh, that's so great, because I just found out that I am, too. We're going to do this together," she said.

As the two women hugged, Trinity let out her own squeal. The only thing more perfect than her special day, and having Drew as her husband, was going through her pregnancy with Jasmine.

"I haven't told Drew yet, so you can't say anything," Trinity said.

"I haven't told Derek either, so we'd both better do it tonight. You know we aren't going to be able to contain ourselves."

They walked out of the room and neither of them noticed the enamored looks on their husband's faces.

* * *

"I never thought I could be this happy," Drew said as he watched Trinity walk toward him.

"Trust me, cousin, I know what you mean," Derek replied.

The men split apart and took their women into their arms. Guests threw birdseed as Trinity and Drew raced to the safety of the back seat of the waiting limo. Trinity was laughing as they collapsed inside, and Drew couldn't get enough of her pure joy and beauty.

"I have one final surprise for you, Trinity."

"I can't imagine anything else."

"We're taking a three-day honeymoon. I wanted it to be longer, but I know neither of us can stand to be away from Cindi too long."

"You know me so well. But I hope it's not too far."

As she continued to kiss him, he groaned.

"You're killing me, woman."

He ran his hand up her thigh, unable not to feel smug when she gasped.

When they arrived at his jet, Drew didn't want to sit down and buckle up. He wanted to lie down and… He wanted to show her how much she meant to him.

Sadly, they did the right thing and buckled up for takeoff.

But her eyes bored into him. "I have something to tell you," she said.

He waited. His hand rubbed up and down her thigh, going higher with each pass he made.

"OK, Drew. We're going to have another baby."

His hand stilled.

"Really?" He was too stunned to think of anything more intelligent to say.

She nodded, and he threw off his seat belt and knelt in front of her. She was having his child, again. He hadn't thought that his life could get any better, but it had.

"You need to buckle back up. We're moving."

With great reluctance, Drew sat back in his seat and buckled up just as the jet started lifting into the air. He couldn't keep his hands off his wife, though. The second the pilots told him they could remove their seat belts, Drew threw his off and pulled her from her seat. He lifted her into his arms and carried her to the large bedroom in the back of the plane.

He laid her on the bed and lifted her dress away so he could caress her stomach.

"I can't believe I'm going to watch you grow from the very beginning. I hate how much I missed out on with Cindi."

"I'm sorry, Drew."

"You have nothing to be sorry about. I can admit I was narrow-minded, and you had every right not to trust me."

"I just hate how much time we lost," she said with tears glistening in her eyes.

"Me too, love. But, what matters now is that we have forever together."

They started kissing again, and all thoughts were erased from their minds as passion quickly took over. And every time was a new beginning.

They fell into an exhausted sleep, and neither of them woke up until the announcement that it was time to buckle up again.

Trinity gasped in delight when she realized where they were. The jet turned in a large circle and landed on the small strip with no extra room to spare.

"I can't believe you brought us back here. You're such a romantic, Mr. Titan," Trinity said with a huge smile.

"I'll make sure we leave together this time," Drew told her.

They headed to the resort and rushed up to the suite where their story began. This time, it would end with a much happier ever-after.

Read the next installment in the
Baby for the Billionaire Series

THE TYCOON'S PROPOSAL

PROLOGUE

RYAN TITAN LOOKED around his empty home with satisfaction. He'd watched his two cousins settle down over the last couple of years, going from Seattle's most eligible bachelors to happily married men, and now he was left feeling like he was missing something.

His cousins, Derek and Drew, were far more like brothers to him than cousins. They'd been raised next to each other and had all gone from poverty level to billionaire status together. They'd each done separate things in the business world but stayed by each other's sides as they climbed to the top of the world's richest ranks.

Ryan felt a bit excluded as he watched his cousins find their true loves, leaving him behind for once. He was always welcome in their homes, but now it was different. He was actually filled with envy as he watched them with their families.

There he stood in a new house without furniture. He shook his head as he wandered around the rooms, his steps echoing off the bare walls. He heard a knock at the door and heard it opening.

"Ryan, where are you?"

"I'm coming," he called back, as he heard the voice of his nephew. Jacob rounded the corner, and the breath was pushed out of Ryan's body, as his thirteen-year-old "nephew" hurled himself into his arms.

"This place is great, Uncle Ryan," Jacob said with enthusiasm. He raced off to check out the home. Ryan was glad he'd bought a place so close to his cousins because Jacob and the rest of his "nieces" and "nephews" could come over anytime.

"Nice place, Ryan," Derek said as he joined them.

"I'm lucky to have found a place so close to you and Drew. I already mapped out the backyard, and we can make a trail between the properties. Then the kids can ride four-wheelers back and forth. We can make a killer trail for all of us," Ryan said. He was excited to get started on the project. There would be no need for fences between the properties.

"Great thinking, cousin. You map it all out, and I'll get the people in to forge the trail," Derek replied.

"Hey, maybe I don't want to tear up my yard. What if I want to keep you hooligans out?" Drew entered the room and jumped into the conversation. Both cousins ignored him, knowing he didn't mean a word of it.

"Where are the ladies?" Ryan asked. He'd expected them to be right behind their husbands.

"They're taking a spa day today. The young ones are at my house," Derek answered.

"They're already spectacular and in no way need to go to the spa," Ryan told them. Both cousins nodded, as they worshiped their wives. However, they would go to the ends of the earth for them and give them absolutely anything they wanted.

"When are you going to finally settle down?" Derek asked him.

"You know me. I don't want a lady coming into my life and messing with a good thing," Ryan said. His typical arrogant smile was on his face, but there was no real meaning behind his words. He was thinking that being single wasn't as great as it had once been. As he looked around at his empty home, he thought it would be pretty great to share it with someone.

He shook off his melancholy mood and showed his cousins around. Unbelievably, the home was even larger than his two cousins' homes. He hadn't planned on the huge place, but the location was what sold him. He wanted to be near his cousins. The older he got, the more he wanted to slow down a bit.

Ryan was a phenomenal architect and remodeled historic homes, which was a hobby for him and not his main career. He'd made his first million in the stock market and his first billion through his many business investments. He had more money than he could ever spend in a lifetime and, although he spent a lot of time in the office still, he took off when he wanted to so he could pursue his love of historic properties.

Ryan called his secretary and gave her free rein on getting his house furnished. Then he headed to the backyard with his cousins so they could plan the quad trail. The rest of the day flew by, and Ryan forgot all about his troubles.

CHAPTER ONE

NICOLE LANDER PARKED her car, saying a prayer of thanks that it had once again made it home. She was grateful each time she turned the key and the engine decided to turn over and work for another day.

She climbed the broken staircase, careful to not lean against the rusted out railing. She'd made that mistake once and had almost fallen through. The only thing that saved her had been her great reflexes.

She reached her door, inserted the key, and spent the next couple of minutes wiggling it around until it finally grasped the mechanisms inside the knob and turned. She rushed inside, quickly relocking the door. She breathed a sigh of relief as she entered the safety of her apartment. She'd seriously be in trouble if someone was ever chasing her because she certainly wouldn't be able to get inside quickly enough to save herself.

Nicole looked around the worn out studio apartment in disgust. It was sparsely furnished with secondhand furniture which had seen much better days. She tried to make her place as homey as possible, but with her very limited budget, there wasn't very much she could do. She opened her refrigerator, only to spot the empty shelves and shut it back up. She was exhausted and only had a few hours to sleep before she had to report to her temporary job.

She was so exhausted she could barely stand on her feet. She was working about twenty hours a day, six days a week, plus a few hours on her seventh day. She couldn't wait until she found a permanent, full-time job so she could actually have some decent hours. Between her jobs and visiting with her sister in the hospital, she knew she looked like a complete wreck.

She fell face first on her bed and wasn't happy when her telephone woke her up a short hour later. She crawled from the bed to pick it up because she knew it had to be important. "Hello," she croaked into the phone.

"We're looking for Nicole Lander," said the voice on the other end of the line.

"This is Nicole. How can I help you?" She replied, a bit more awake.

"We've pre-screened you for a full-time job and think you'd be perfect for the position," the woman said.

Nicole was on instant alert. "I'd love to hear about it," she told the woman.

"The position is for a live-in housekeeper. You'd be provided room and board, plus a generous salary if you're interested in coming in for an interview."

"I'll be there whenever you need me to be," Nicole said, without needing to ask any questions. She didn't care if she scrubbed toilets all day, as long as she could get out of her current flat. "When do you want me?"

"You need to come into the office and fill out some paperwork. Confidentiality is a must while working for this client. You'll have to sign papers attesting to the fact that you won't speak about what happens in the household. You'll also be required to submit to a drug test. Your background check is already complete. If you come into the office this afternoon, we can interview you. I want to let you know there are a few other people interested."

"I'll be down there in a half hour. I have no problem signing whatever you need," Nicole told her. She hoped she wasn't sounding too desperate.

"That sounds great, Nicole. I'll be waiting for you," she said before disconnecting the call. Nicole thought the client must be one of those wealthy hermits who didn't like the world to see them. She really didn't care. Her temp company wouldn't send her to an unsafe place. Even if her room was tiny, it would be better than the studio in which she currently resided. She was on the verge of losing the place, anyway, because her sister's hospital bills were depleting her bank account.

Even though she hadn't gotten enough sleep, she was wired with excitement running through her veins. She jumped into the shower and made it to the offices in just under thirty minutes. She walked from the interview, confident she'd be selected. By the time she got back home and crawled into bed, sleep overtook her and she felt some peace, which she hadn't felt in far too long.

When she got the call the next day, she hung her head and barely managed to hold the tears back. Someone else had gotten the position. She was running out of options. She didn't know how she was going to take care of Patsy's hospital bills and still keep a roof over their heads. She got dressed and headed toward her waitressing job, where she'd be lucky to take home thirty dollars in tips for a ten-hour shift. It wasn't much motivation, but it was better than nothing.

* * *

Three months later, Nicole sat by her phone, trying to work up her courage. She had to call him. There was no other choice. Nicole was cringing at the thought of groveling at Ryan Titan's feet, but she really didn't see any other options. Her sister needed the operation and, as hard as Nicole worked, she still couldn't pay for it. The hospital didn't care if it was a life or death matter. They only cared about the bottom line. She couldn't believe they said it was an elective surgery. It was something slowly killing her, though--not an emergency. They wouldn't perform it without payment in full.

Nicole took a deep breath, her hand resting on the phone. She'd been in the same position for the last hour, trying to force herself to pick it up. Her palms were sweaty, and her heart was beating irregularly--out of control. The tear tracks down her cheeks had long since dried, but the terror was still there.

She hadn't talked to Ryan in twelve years, and their last conversation hadn't gone well. He still believed she'd cheated on him. It had been so much easier to let him believe that, but oh how it had broken her heart.

She told herself repeatedly it wasn't about her. It was about her little sister, and no matter how much he may hate her, he'd always loved Patsy. There was no way he'd sit back and let her die when he could help her.

She wiped her hands on her jeans and picked up the handle of the phone, trying to control her trembling hands. She had to redial the number three times. She was shaking so hard she kept punching the wrong numbers.

As the phone started to ring, her nerves reached the breaking point. She was hoping it would go to voicemail. Then she could just leave a message and not have to face hearing his voice.

"Who is this?" a voice demanded, startling her.

"Th… this is Nicole," she stuttered. There was an uncomfortably long pause on the other end of the line.

"Nicole who?" came the same voice, as cool as ice.

"Nicole Lander," she said, barely above a whisper.

"How did you get my personal number?" he demanded. She was thinking she'd made a really bad mistake. It sounded as if he didn't even remember who she was. Maybe their time together had been far more significant to her than it had been to him.

"I got it from your uncle," she finally managed to say. There was another really long silence at her words.

"What do you want?" he demanded.

"I…um…wanted to see if I could…um…talk to you about something important," she forced through her trembling lips. "We used to know each other a really long time ago. I don't know if you still remember me," she finished.

"I don't have time to beat around the bush. Spit out what it is you want," he demanded of her. She didn't want to ask him for money over the phone, but what choice did she have?

"My little sister is in the hospital. She needs an operation, and we don't have any other options. Your uncle said I should talk to you," she finally pushed out, on the verge of crying once again. She could tell by his tone of voice he was simply humoring her and, in no way, was he going to help them out. Nicole was going to lose her baby sister, and she didn't think she could possibly make it through the horrific experience.

He was silent for so long she thought he'd hung up the phone. Ryan didn't remember Nicole or her sister, and he was far too important a man to sit there on the phone with her. She'd failed her last resort and she felt an overwhelming sense of grief. She was starting to take the phone from her ear when he finally spoke again.

"Do you know where my office is?"

"Yes, in the city," she mumbled.

"Be there tomorrow at five," he said, and then she heard nothing but a dial tone.

Nicole sat there for a couple of minutes, in shock, as the phone continued to beep at her. She finally managed to hang up and allowed the tears to fall down her cheeks. It wasn't hopeless. Ryan was willing to hear her out. She didn't care what it took. Nicole had to convince him to help her baby sister. She couldn't lose her.

* * *

Ryan sat at his desk, feeling a myriad of emotions coursing through him. He'd known who was on the other end of his line from the very first word she'd whispered. He could never forget that voice. It had haunted his dreams for the past twelve years. She'd been the girl who got away. Hell, not only got away, but thrust him from her life.

He ran his hands through his hair and let out a sigh of frustration. How he wished he could've simply told her to go to hell and hung up the phone, but there was no way he could be that much of a bastard. He'd loved Patsy as if she was his own little sister.

He felt a smile lift the corner of his lips, as he thought back to little Patsy toddling around his legs as he spent time with Nicole. She had become attached to him from the very first moment he came through her doors. Over the years he'd watched her grow up, she'd squeezed a piece of his heart.

Ryan hadn't heard Patsy was hurt. He decided to make some calls and get some background information on the situation. He needed to be well prepared when Nicole stepped through his doors. He'd been incredibly surprised by her call. He wasn't having any more surprises when she stepped back into his life. He also needed to speak to his uncle. He didn't know what the old man was up to, but he knew not to give his number out to anyone. His uncle should've taken her number and given it to Ryan. That way he wouldn't have been surprised. He didn't like to be blindsided.

By the time Ryan got the answers he was looking for, he hung his head in shame. He couldn't believe how bad things had gotten for Patsy. He knew beyond any shadow of a doubt he'd help her, but Nicole didn't know that. He'd help Patsy, but he was also going to get what he wanted from Nicole.

She'd once thought he wasn't good enough for her, and now he was the only one who could save her baby sister. He felt a sense of justice in that knowledge. He knew there wasn't any point in working the rest of the day, as he couldn't concentrate. He was eager for his appointment the next day. A smile stole across his features as he sat back in his chair. He enjoyed a challenge, and Nicole would definitely provide him some entertainment.

He made several phone calls, which included getting Patsy moved to a private room. He then found the best Cardiothoracic surgeon he could find and called him in for a consult. Ryan didn't do anything in half-measures, and he wanted to make sure Patsy received only the best of care.

By the time he hung up the phone, he felt more in control. Patsy was going to be well taken care of, and he was going to get his chance for redemption with Nicole. She'd pay for what she'd done to him, and they'd both enjoy the punishment.

Ryan headed home, feeling better than he had felt in a long while. That somewhat empty feeling he had been dealing with for quite some time seemed to have completely lifted. He found himself smiling as he jogged up the stairs to change clothing. He was meeting up with Drew later in the evening and decided to enjoy his great mood.

* * *

Nicole paced outside the high rise building, working up her courage to enter through the double doors. He wouldn't have told her to come in unless he was going to help her sister. He may hate her for what he thought she'd done to him, but he used to be the kindest person she knew, and there was no way he could let Patsy die.

She squared her shoulders and held her head up high as she entered the plush interior of Titan Enterprises. Even the lobby of the building screamed luxury, with its marble floors and huge security desk. There were plants strategically placed to make the area warm and inviting, and several people were moving around the lobby, coming in and out of different doors. Nicole didn't know if the room was supposed to seem intimidating or not, but it certainly made her feel out of place. The people he dealt with on a daily basis most likely didn't notice the luxury surrounding them, as they were around it all the time.

The guard behind the desk looked pleasant enough, but Nicole could see the steel in his gaze. If she wasn't on the acceptable list, there was no way she'd make it to the elevators. She had to fight every instinct in her, which told her to turn around and run away. She was made stronger than that and wouldn't back down. She'd fought harder battles in her life, but her sister's surgery was the only one she'd ever fought with her whole being.

She tried to walk with as much confidence as she could muster. What if having her come in had been nothing but a cruel joke, and the guard was going to send her on her way? If that was the case, she'd leave kicking and screaming. There was nothing she wouldn't do for her sister, even if it meant humiliating herself.

"Do you have an appointment?" the man asked.

"Yes, I'm here to see Mr. Titan," she answered. She'd been trying to sound confident, but her throaty voice sounded weak, even to her own ears. She took a few deep breaths, trying to pull herself together.

"Your name, please?" the guard asked.

"Nicole Lander." The man looked at his computer for a moment, and she had to quell the rising panic. After what seemed an inordinately long time, though it was only seconds, he nodded his head and handed her a badge.

"Go to the elevators and swipe this badge. Go up to the twentieth floor. When you step off the elevators, go to the right, and you'll find the reception desk. Mr. Titan is expecting you, so check in with his secretary," the man said. Nicole nodded at him to let him know she understood.

Walking over to the elevators, she pushed the button and waited. It felt like she was in a fog as the bell chimed and the doors opened. She stepped inside and had to fight her claustrophobia as the metal machine rose higher and higher. Instead of feeling comforted by the music, she felt more closed in. She hated small places. As the numbers lit up, signaling her imminent arrival, she could feel her breathing become shallower. She was seconds away from seeing her first love, and she had a feeling the meeting would be quite chilling.

She'd wanted him to hate her when she pushed him out of her life. It had been a far better option than the alternative. There was no way she wanted him to know who she really was. She'd much rather have him look at her with anger and contempt in his eyes than pity or disgust from knowing the truth.

The doors opened, and she jumped a bit when the bell signaled her arrival. On wooden legs, she stepped from the doors and made her way to the beautiful desk, which sat in the middle of a huge reception area.

"Name, please?" the woman asked, barely looking up from her computer.

"Nicole Lander," she answered in a voice that was a bit stronger than the one she'd used with the security guard. The woman picked up her phone and spoke into it for a moment.

"Mr. Titan is currently busy. He asked me to tell you to have a seat. He'll call you when he's finished up," the woman said. She turned back to her computer, confident Nicole would do what she was told.

Nicole walked over to one of the plush seats and picked up a magazine. She glanced at her watch every few minutes. She was anxious to get back. She really wanted to make it to the hospital to visit with her sister before she had to report in to her waitressing job.

The time continued to tick by, and she was seething mad once an hour had passed. She figured she'd be in his office for no more than a half hour, but if she didn't get in there soon she wouldn't be able to visit her sister. She stepped up to the desk, thinking he'd forgotten about her.

"I wanted to make sure Mr. Titan knew I was still here," she said to the receptionist. She knew she had a bit of bite to her tone, but it was rude to make someone wait this long. He must assume he was the only one who had a life. The secretary looked up, startled, like she couldn't possibly believe Nicole would dare to question her boss's intentions.

"Mr. Titan's a very busy man. You'll have to wait for him to call you in," the woman rudely replied. Nicole nodded and took her seat again. Another half hour passed, still with no word from Ryan, and she could no longer wait. She couldn't afford to be late to her job. It looked like he'd played her for a fool. He was most likely in his office, watching her fidget from some hidden camera and having a nice laugh to himself.

She slowly got up and headed off toward the elevator. She didn't approach the reception desk again. Why bother? She took the elevator back downstairs and returned the badge to the security guard. She held her head high as she exited the building. She was going to barely make it to work on time, so she wouldn't allow the tears--that were trying so hard to escape—to fall.

She felt like she had failed her baby sister. She really didn't see any other options of being able to pay the surgery bill. She'd already given up her tiny apartment. She was living on friends' couches and her sister's hospital room chair. She had sold everything of value she owned, and it still wasn't enough. Her car decided when it wanted to work, which was only about half the time. She wasn't a person to give up on anything, but she didn't see what more she could possibly do.

She rushed in the doors of the second rate, all-night truck stop where she waitressed and put her purse away. She made it out to the floor with a minute to spare. Her boss looked up with a glare and pointedly glanced at the clock. He then went back to his paper and ignored her. It was going to be a long night, as she hadn't gotten a decent night's sleep in forever. She was used to that and would deal with it like she did everything thrown her way.

* * *

Ryan hadn't expected the business call to take so long and was about to pull his hair out when he finally managed to get off the phone. He'd been planning on making Nicole wait for a while, just to make sure she squirmed in her seat a bit. He wasn't normally so rude, though, as to make someone wait two hours.

"You can send Ms. Lander in now," he said into his intercom.

There was a pause before his efficient secretary came back. "It looks as if she left," came the reply. Ryan didn't say anything else. He hung up and called the security desk asking if she'd left the building, only to find out she'd indeed left about a half hour earlier. She wasn't acting like someone who wanted a favor. If any other person had walked out before he was ready to speak with them he would've scrapped the whole thing, but this wasn't business. It was personal.

He made some phone calls and found out where she was. When he discovered where she was working, his bad mood deepened even further. He really shouldn't give a damn where she worked or what she did. She shouldn't matter to him in the least, but when he thought about her working overnight at that dive of a truck stop, his stomach clenched. He knew the kind of people who habituated a place like that in the wee hours of the morning, and it was certainly no place for a woman.

He gathered up his things and called his driver. It looked like he was dining out that night. He smiled to himself when he pictured her reaction to him entering the joint. Hell, when his car pulled up, he was sure there would be a bit of a stir. People like him simply didn't go to places like that. At least, people like he was nowadays. He would've been happy to go anywhere when he was a kid. That would've been a real treat.

It took the driver about forty minutes to navigate traffic and pull up in front of the diner. It was fairly busy, and he looked through the windows, spotting her almost immediately. She'd changed in the years since he'd seen her last, but not much.

Her young, sleek body had matured and now she had curves, though he couldn't see them well beneath the loose clothing and apron she was wearing. Her hair was still dark and hung low on her back in an unflattering braid, which looked like she had made it up in minutes.

As he stepped through the diner doors and quickly browsed, he could see the weariness in her movements. When she finally turned to see who'd walked in and caused a silence to fall over her customers, he felt a kick in his gut by the sheer exhaustion of her expression.

She'd always been so full of life, and now she looked drained, as if she bore the weight of the world on her shoulders. She approached him slowly, looking at him as if he was a dangerous animal ready to strike any moment. His lips turned up in a sardonic smile because he was a dangerous animal--far more deadly than any four-legged creatures she might ever encounter.

"Do you want a table?" she asked him suspiciously.

"That would be great," he responded overconfidently.

"What would you like to drink?" she asked through clenched teeth.

"I'll take a coffee," he replied. He'd determined within minutes of walking in that she'd be leaving with him. He knew exactly what he wanted as payment for helping her sister. He'd enjoy a bit of cat and mouse in the meantime. He knew he'd win, so he could be indulgent for a while.

"Here's the menu. I'll be right back with your coffee," she said and walked off. He enjoyed the sway of her hips, which were slightly thicker than they had been when they were teenagers. She'd definitely turned into a woman, and he couldn't wait to explore the new her. She was still stunning, even with the stress and exhaustion etched into her features.

She returned with the coffee, and he noticed the mirth in her eyes as he took his first sip and a grimace passed over his features. It was horrible, and he had the feeling she was enjoying his suffering. He controlled his face and took another long sip, just so he could wipe that smug look off her face. She looked as if she was trying to control her expression, but she couldn't hide the twinkle in her gorgeous brown eyes.

"Are you ready to place your order?"

"What are your specials?" he asked in a serious tone. He enjoyed watching her try and act nonchalant with him, though she wasn't doing nearly as great of a job as she thought she was.

"We have the chef's meatloaf special, and we serve breakfast all day," she said sweetly. He perused the menu, like he really cared what he ordered. Her foot started tapping impatiently as she continued to wait for him.

"Ms. Lander, can you please come over here?" Ryan heard her boss call. He noticed the twinge she couldn't stop from crossing her features.

"Yes, Mr. Archer," she said, with a long look at Ryan before she turned.

Ryan watched her walk over to where her boss was standing and strained his ears to hear their conversation.

"Could you please try and act more professional? That man showed up in a Jaguar, and you're tapping your toe in impatience. Do you want to keep your job?" Nicole's boss threatened.

"Of course, sir. I'm sorry about that," Ryan heard her say. Her voice was subdued.

Her boss dismissed her, and Nicole walked back over to Ryan, fury evident in her eyes.

"I'm sorry about making you wait. Have you decided yet?"

she asked him.

"I'll take a turkey sandwich and the soup of the day," he responded. Ryan didn't like the way her boss had spoken to her, and it only solidified his decision she'd be leaving with him. She jotted down his order and quickly disappeared.

Nicole served him his food quickly, and he forced himself to choke some of it down while he continued to watch her. She never stopped running as she refilled coffee and took down orders. She kept his glass topped off, along with those of the other twenty or so customers. He almost came out of his seat when he saw some trucker get a little bit too friendly. Ryan had to admit he was impressed how she handled the man, letting him know she was unavailable, while still being polite.

Ryan gave up on eating the terrible food and sat back, drinking the muddy coffee. He'd been there for a couple of hours, and several of the customers cleared out, and yet she was still running around. Her boss snapped orders at her left and right, and Nicole still managed to keep a positive attitude. She had to be dead on her feet.

Ryan wasn't going to take much more. "We need to talk," he told her when she came to top off his mug again.

"I can't talk right now. I'm working," she told him, somewhat exasperated.

"Have you had a break yet tonight?"

She looked at him as if he was insane. She was lucky to get to run to the bathroom on any given night. "I'm the only waitress here. I don't have time to take a break," she finally said and turned to walk away.

He grabbed her wrist and pulled her into the booth next to him. She gasped in outrage at his high-handedness.

"Ms. Lander, you have customers waiting for you," her boss said, thinking she was slacking on the job.

She looked at Ryan in a panic. If he was trying to get her fired, he was doing an excellent job. "I'm sorry, sir. I tripped," she said as she struggled to get back up.

"Ms. Lander hasn't had a break the entire time I've been here, and I'd like to speak to her for a few minutes," Ryan said to the man, glaring over at him.

"I don't appreciate you telling me how to treat my employees, as it's none of your business." Nicole's boss puffed up in anger. "Get back to work, Ms. Lander," he snapped.

She once again struggled to get up, but Ryan still refused to let her go. You're going to get me fired," she said through gritted teeth. She was starting to get scared. He could see the vulnerability in her eyes. He was done with the place, and she was leaving with him, even if he had to throw her over his shoulder.

"We're leaving now," he said as he released her and stood up. He threw some bills on the table and grabbed his jacket. Nicole quickly fled from him, then went around the tables and refilled her customers' glasses. He stood by the counter and waited until she was done.

"I need to use the restroom. I'll be right back," Nicole told her boss and quickly disappeared. Ryan's rage increased when the man nodded tightly. He couldn't believe she needed to get permission to use the bathroom. It was ridiculous. He spotted the cook, who looked like an understanding man.

He pulled a couple hundred from his pocket and approached the guy. "Can you please grab Nicole's things for me? She's leaving with me now, whether she wants to or not, and I think she'd rather have her possessions," Ryan said to the guy, who sized him up. "I won't harm her. Our families have been friends since childhood, and she'll no longer need this job," he assured the cook.

"She should've left here long ago. The boss treats her like crap," the cook said. He grabbed her belongings and set them on the counter, then stood waiting for Nicole to come out. She appeared quickly, since it seemed she wasn't allowed more than a couple of minutes, even to use the restroom.

"Nicole, do you know this guy?" the cook asked.

Her shoulders seemed to sag a bit as she tried to figure out how to answer that question. "We grew up together. Don't worry, Bubba, he's not trying to hurt me," she assured the cook. She had no clue she'd just given the cook permission to let Ryan cart her out of the restaurant, or she would've never said that. Bubba smiled at Ryan and gave him the thumbs up.

"Right then, let's go," he told Nicole once again.

"Ryan, I already told you I'm not going anywhere with you. I don't get off until eight in the morning," she almost yelled at him. She then looked over at her boss, who was glaring at her. "If you really want to talk to me, I'll come to your offices in the morning."

Ryan didn't feel the need to talk anymore. He grabbed her things up, then grabbed her around the waist and tossed her over his shoulder and started walking toward the front door.

The Tycoon's Proposal is available at all major retailers.

27778407R00138

Made in the USA
San Bernardino, CA
17 December 2015